I0789014

Monarch
Book Six of Claire Lance

Geonn Cannon

Supposed Crimes LLC • Matthews, North Carolina

Published in the United States.

ISBN: 978-1-952150-13-5

Cover Image
Sarah Deakins, photographed by WendyD Photography for the film
Last Stand to Nowhere.
With gratitude to Michelle Muldoon

www.supposedcrimes.com

This book is typeset in Goudy Old Style.

Chapter One

NOTHING COULD really prepare a person to live in a tourist trap. Even if it was a lovely one, as lovely as December Harbor, it was hard to ignore the façade. Residents were bombarded by constant reminders that they lived in a town which existed mostly for other people to visit. The main streets were full of tacky souvenir shops and quaint inns catering to people drawn to the island, hoping to catch a glimpse of the killer whales that live next door in the Strait of Georgia.

The tourists came by ferry, private boat, planes, and small cruise ships. They boosted the island's population by a few hundred for a few hours at a time, treating it like their own private playground while the permanent residents become background players in their own homes. They clogged the streets of downtown, wander into traffic, brought their obnoxious trucks and station wagons, turned quiet restaurants into crowded hotspots. They drove up along the coast to Sholeh Village and climbed onto boats to go whale-watching. They headed to the airport and rent a helicopter for sightseeing tours of the island and its surrounding archipelago.

Then, eventually, the weather cooled, and the infestation took care of itself. Once winter moved in, even the idyllic weather of Squire's Isle turned cold and wet enough to dissuade even the hardiest of vacationers until only the true islands survived.

Deputy Claire Curran considered all of this as she sat behind the wheel of her cruiser with a cup of lukewarm coffee and counted the cars coming off the afternoon ferry. Only twelve today, not counting the service and delivery vehicles. She craned her neck to look at the overcast sky. The cloud cover was low enough to imitate fog. The air had a navy-blue sheen, and the shops on either side of Spring Street looked gilded by the light shining through their windows.

She didn't miss the tourists. The crowds and the traffic, the noise of the sightseeing tour chopper zipping by overhead every ninety minutes or so. But she did have to admit the off-season could be very incredibly boring.

The radio chirped, and she traded the coffee for the handset. There was a short burst of static and then dispatcher Minnie Culpepper's voice came over the speaker.

"Yoo-hoo, you out there listening, Car Two?"

Claire smiled. "I'm here, Min. What have you got for me?"

"Sheriff wants to talk with you. Nothing important, he just wants to make sure you'll be back at the barn at four o'clock."

"I was planning on it." She looked at the time. "Is everything okay?"

Minnie said, "As far as I know, but you folks never tell me anything around here."

"Because half the time you already know it."

"That implies gossipry and snooping, and I'm going to hang up so you don't hear how offended I am. Stay warm, Deputy Claire."

"Tell Cal I'll be there. And I'll bring you some crullers when I come in."

"I might forgive you."

Claire chuckled quietly as she hung up the handset. Down the street, the ferry had finished unloading and was now being filled by cars heading back to the mainland. She'd spent her entire life landlocked, with Lake Michigan being the closest thing she'd ever seen to an ocean, but she'd been on Squire's Isle long enough to know this rhythm. It was as regular and predictable as clockwork.

Tide comes in; tide goes out.

She finished her coffee, checked the time again, and decided to head in a little early. She was only two blocks from the station and could probably have jogged there as fast as driving, but the wind rocked the car and reminded her why that would be a very poor idea.

Besides, she'd promised Minnie some doughnuts.

***

The sheriff's office shared a simple but sprawling yellow building with the courthouse, the two sides connected at the hip by the jailhouse. It was a simple, plain building, but Claire was fond of the station. It had a series of nine-paned windows facing the street and a stately clock tower separating the law from the order. It was just at the edge of the tourism district and marked the beginning of what she considered the town proper. It was here one might find banks, salons, and the random necessities for people who called the island home year-round.

She left the car in the back lot and went inside. The bullpen was a large single room with a row of glass-fronted offices along one wall. Six desks were in the center of the room, even though there were only three full-time officers on the payroll, and Claire went to the one she'd staked out as hers. She could see Sheriff Cal Rucker in his office, standing with a shoulder against the wall rather than seated at his desk.

Minnie was manning her post at the long counter separating the public area from the bullpen, but she spun in her seat to face Claire. No one had ever told her the woman's age, but she'd seemed absolutely ancient when Claire joined the department. In the seven years since, she seemed to have somehow become younger and more energetic. Today she wore a thick black sweater with a strange white flower blooming from her left shoulder.

"I went ahead and marked you as off-duty."

"Thanks, Min." She nodded toward the sheriff. "Is he okay? He seems..."

"Maudlin? Yepper. He's been real quiet all day. He's barely said two words to me since he started his shift, and most of those were 'be sure Deputy Curran stops by to talk to me before she ends her shift.' So consider my job done, hon."

Claire hummed under her breath and gave Minnie the bag of crullers she'd gotten from Coffee Table Books.

"You're going to ruin my dinner."

"I don't think you're complaining."

Minnie shrugged and pulled out a doughnut as she spun her chair back around.

Claire crossed the room and knocked on Rucker's door. He straightened, not startled, and turned slowly to face her. He held up a hand to motion her in with two fingers. His uniform was neatly-pressed as always, but there was a hint of grey-white stubble on his chin and at his temples. The top of his head was, as always, shiny and smooth.

"Anything exciting today?" he asked when she came into the office.

"Nothing out of the ordinary. Gave a ticket to a guy for going forty-five in a twenty-five. There was a broken taillight this morning. It's the nice and quiet season."

Rucker made a quiet noise under his breath. Claire watched him and tried to read his body language.

"Is everything okay, Ruck?"

"Mm," he said, looking down at his shoes. Finally, he looked up again. "We need to talk, Claire. Not here, though. Somewhere... uh... the city park. They have those bleachers. We can talk there."

She gestured at the chair in front of his desk. "We can't talk here?"

"I'd rather not."

"Are you worried about Minnie gossiping?"

He looked past her and managed to chuckle. "Always. But no, I just think this is something we need to talk about away from this place."

"Should I be worried?"

"I don't think so. Oh! No. No, I'm not... this isn't..." He waved his hand. "I'm not firing you or anything like that."

She felt some of the tension leave her shoulders. "Okay, then."

"Do you have the time? Is your wife expecting you to come home, or do you have plans or..."

"I have time for a conversation, Ruck. You obviously have something you need to get off your chest. So let's go have a talk."

He nodded and took his coat from the back of his chair. "Yeah. Okay, Claire. Let's go have a talk."

***

They took separate cars to the park so Claire could go directly home after their talk. She waited until the cruiser pulled out in front of her and followed him through town. The sky had grown darker while she was inside, and by the time they arrived at their destination, they had to rely on the security lights shining at either side of the block to see.

Rucker led her halfway up the bleachers, bent down to brush away any dirt or frost that might have accumulated on the metal, and took a seat with a low groan. Claire sat next to him and waited.

"Looks like snow, probably."

Claire looked up at the sky. "Yeah, probably. Is that your years of wisdom speaking, or did you hear the forecast on the radio this morning like I did?"

He laughed softly, just a quick exhale of air through his nostrils. Ghostly-white smoke wafted around in front of his face before being carried away on the breeze.

"Probably the second one." He leaned forward with his elbows on his knees and looked out across the empty field. "I'm old, Claire. Getting older every day."

"Ideally, that's the way it works."

"Sure, sure. But I'm *old*." This time he put extra emphasis on the word. "I was old when I started this job, and that was a long, long time ago. So long ago that I've seen this entire island evolve into a completely different place. We were a conservative town. There were no rainbow flags in businesses, certainly no Pride parade on Spring Street. I was there when the change started; I saw it happening in real time." He laughed and sat up straighter. "I never thought this town would ever have a woman as mayor, let alone one with a wife."

He fell silent, but Claire waited. She knew Rucker supported the gay community on the island, so she wasn't worried about where the conversation might lead, but she was definitely curious and confused. She was also freezing and eager to discover the purpose of this talk.

"Something's coming. I'm not talking about the snow, or something you might have heard on the forecast. This is something else, and I don't think I'm the person who should be in charge of protecting the island when it hits. And I also don't want to step down without having a replacement I can trust ready to take over."

"You can't appoint anyone. There has to be an election..."

"Yeah, yeah," he said, waving his hand dismissively. "There will be an election, and I'll say 'you should vote for whoever,' and everyone who used to vote for me will vote for that person instead. I'd really like for that person to be you, Claire."

She sat up straighter and looked down at her hands. "Ruck, I'm not sure that's the best idea."

"I have to disagree."

"I have a past."

"We all have a past. Hell, I had a past when I first got the job. You've been the deputy here for six years. People know you. They trust you. They like you. They like you more than they like me. And to be honest, I was thinking about this day when you walked into my office and told me who you were and why you wanted a job."

Claire said, "Randall has seniority. If anyone—"

"Randall would laugh in my face if I offered him the job. His first priority is his wife, and if he was sheriff, he wouldn't be able to take extra vacation days for her doctor's appointments. He's happy right where he is."

"You've already talked to him about this."

"Of course. He has seniority." He smiled at her. "It was all hypothetical, of course, but he was very emphatic in his support."

She rubbed her hands together. "I have time to think about it, right? You're not thinking about hanging your hat up tomorrow, right?"

"Oh, sure, sure..." He squinted into the distance and nodded slowly, unconvincingly. "Yeah. You should talk it over with Jodie. See what she has to say. But I think we both know her well enough to make a pretty good guess. Here's the bottom line, Claire. I'm not going to be the sheriff here very much longer. Someone has to take over. It's either going to be you or some stranger. Probably someone brought in from the mainland. I hate the idea of that. I know you do, too."

He pushed himself up with a grunt. "Having our talk here was a very dumb idea. One more sign that I should have quit a long time ago."

Claire stood next to him. "Is everything okay, Ruck? You didn't get bad news from a check-up or anything like that."

He laughed and clapped a hand on her shoulder. "No, nothing like that. I promise. Just... getting my ducks in a row. You don't have anything to worry about."

She nodded uncertainly.

"Come on, let's get out of here."

"Do you want to come over? Jodie won't be home yet, but I can whip you up something for dinner."

Rucker shook his head. "No, no, I should get back to the office. Deal with some of that dreaded paperwork you're going to be cursing about soon enough."

"Something to look forward to."

They walked to the parking lot together, splitting up to go to their own cars. When Claire pulled out of the parking lot, Rucker's car was still parked in the spot where she'd left him. The security light cast an unnaturally bright beam through the windshield and cast him in the perfect silhouette. She couldn't help but think of how vulnerable it made him look.

She bleeped her horn. His head lifted, he waved her away, and then started his car. Claire didn't want him to think she was babysitting him, so she returned his wave and pulled out of the lot toward home.

***

Home had an actual white picket fence, though any attempts at a garden died in the very early stages. It was a split-level house on the fringes of the town proper, a short walk from the wild interior of the island. Rent was cheaper here, as if living near the woods was somehow worth less than having a water view. They had the occasional deer and rabbit visitor, but Claire considered that a bonus when the realtor first mentioned it.

The upper part of the house was blue shingles, the lower half white siding. Even now, having lived there for six years, a quiet voice said *this is your home* when her headlights swept across the front lawn. It was a vaguely alien feeling, even now, but she found it freeing rather than claustrophobic. She spent a long time looking for a home, and this was finer than any she could have dreamed up.

The windows were dark, as expected. She parked in front of the garage and let herself in through the side door. She unfastened her holster and returned her gun to the safe, unsure why she even bothered to carry it. She'd never even considered drawing it the entire time she'd been with the department, and Rucker admitted that his had probably only left the holster five times since he became sheriff. The island wasn't that sort of place. Violent crimes didn't happen. There were robberies, domestic assaults, but she honestly couldn't imagine a scenario that would be improved by being armed.

Maybe that was something she'd change when she was sheriff. If she became sheriff. No. Of course she was going to accept his offer.

Wasn't she?

The thought risked sending her mind in a million different directions, so she changed out of her uniform into a T-shirt and pajama pants, then went into the kitchen to start dinner.

Cooking was a hobby that caught her by surprise. She was used to apartments and small utilitarian kitchens, so takeout was a necessity she'd fallen back on more nights than not. Now she had a full stove, an actual oven, what seemed like acres of counter space, and all kinds of tools and utensils. It seemed wasteful to just let such a big part of their house go unused, so she started exploring.

"Just because you have a home doesn't mean you have to go full domestic," her wife had teased when the first meals began filling up the fridge.

"Just because I cook multiple portions doesn't mean I have to give you some."

Jodie surrendered at that threat, and since then, cooking had become Claire's meditation at the end of the day. She looked in the fridge and gauged what was on hand and how much time she had before Jodie showed up, then began gathering her materials. She made a mixture of Parmesan, salt, paprika, garlic powder, onion powder, and black pepper, coated pork chops with it, and put them in the air fryer. While it cooked, she sliced zucchini and put the rounds on a baking sheet before dressing them with the excess Parmesan mixture and popped them into the oven.

The food was nearly finished when Jodie pulled into the driveway. She breezed into the house a few minutes later, gasping deeply as she crossed the threshold as if she'd been holding her breath the entire time she was gone. Jodie's new shorter hairstyle still made Claire smile. The discovery of gray at her temples had prompted drastic measures: a pair of shears and a new 'do that made her look like James Dean. Claire immediately liked the look, and she'd liked the gray, and she had a feeling she would approve of whatever the next change might be.

Jodie pushed the door shut and returned the smile Claire gave her. "House smells like heaven as usual." She unzipped her jacket and stowed it in the closet. "What's on the menu?"

"Parmesan pork chops with zucchini rounds."

"You're too good to me. I'm so glad I married you before I found out you could cook. Now you know it's really love and I'm not just after your culinary skills."

Claire said, "It's not why you married me, but it's a big part of why you stay."

"The sex is good, too," Jodie said as she came into the kitchen.

"What do you mean 'good'?"

Jodie wrapped her arms around Claire and kissed her hello. "I save my really effusive praise for when I'm in the moment."

Claire grinned. "Yes ma'am, you certainly do."

Jodie slipped out of the embrace and went to the sink. She rolled up her sleeves and began washing up.

"Good day?" Claire asked.

"Fine day," Jodie said. "I was over at Kevin's. He was having trouble with his washer and dryer, so he let me watch him fix it."

"Did you learn anything useful?"

"Oh yeah. I can take apart a washer and put it back together now. I'm not entirely sure it will work afterward. But if it starts screwing up, I think I know enough to save us a maintenance call. You'd be amazed how often the answer is to unplug it and plug it back in again."

Claire grinned. "The answer to so many of life's problems."

"What about you? How was your day?"

Claire honestly wasn't sure if she should tell the whole truth. As far as she knew, Rucker was speaking in hypotheticals about something months in the future. Then again, she and Jodie had never kept anything this big from each other. Jodie dried her hands and set the table. Claire served up their dinner and took a seat across from Jodie.

"Rucker wanted to have a chat with me after I got off-duty."

"Oh, Claire, no. Are you in trouble? Did you get detention?"

Claire smiled. "It sort of felt that way, to be honest. But actually, he wanted to have a conversation about the future. Apparently, he's thinking about retiring."

Jodie's fork froze on the way to her mouth, her eyes unblinking. Claire loved Jodie's eyes; they were multicolored, blue and green, and she'd never seen anything so beautiful. They were Jodie's own personal Northern Lights, and Claire felt honored to look into them at private moments like this.

"Well...?" Jodie prompted.

"Apparently the job is mine if I want it."

Jodie dropped her fork and stood up, leaning across the table to kiss Claire. "Congratulations! That is huge. That is... so, so amazing, Claire. Wow. You're going to be a great sheriff."

"It's not a done deal," Claire reminded her. "Hypothetical. At some future point, when he decides to retire."

Jodie settled back in her seat. "Not to be rude, honey, but it can't be that far off."

Claire grimaced. "He's not that old."

Jodie said, "Honey."

Claire conceded the point, albeit reluctantly. "But the question remains if I'm the right person to take over for him."

"Who else would it be? Why not you?"

"Because of who I am."

Jodie looked confused, then understood. "Because of your past? Your past is what makes you the perfect person for the job. You never did anything wrong. You helped people even when it put you in danger. You saved my life." She reached across the table and Claire met her halfway, taking her hand. "I know the main reason you took my name when we got married was to put distance between yourself and the past. But you're still the same person you were, and the people of this island would be lucky to have someone like you watching out for them."

Claire shrugged.

"Besides, the people who matter already know who you are. Ruck, the mayor, the other officers. If they don't care, you shouldn't worry about it."

"Maybe I should take the job, but do an interview with the paper so everyone knows exactly who they're getting."

Jodie said, "Maybe. I don't think it would change anyone's minds to know you're a hero, but if it helps you sleep better..."

Claire rolled her eyes. "Hero..."

"My hero."

Claire chuckled. "Eat."

Jodie winked at her and focused on her food.

***

After dinner, after watching a TV show on Jodie's laptop, and showering, Claire came out of the bedroom to find Jodie lying seductively across the bed, head propped up on one hand, her nightshirt pulled up to show the full curve of her leg. Claire paused in the bathroom doorway to appreciate the sight before she turned off the light and came closer.

"What's the occasion, Mrs. Curran?"

"I believe my wife told me she's in line to get a very nice promotion, and in my experience, that is worthy of sexual gratification."

Claire plucked at the gym shorts she was wearing. "Well, obviously, that's why I wore my finest lingerie." She got into bed and pulled Jodie to her. "Are you sure you're not just trying to get in good with the next sheriff so you can start your life of crime?"

"I've always wanted to be a bad girl," Jodie said, her mouth already on Claire's lips before she finished speaking.

Claire rolled onto her back and Jodie straddled her, resting her hands on the headboard as Claire kissed her chest through the thin cotton of her shirt. Claire put her arms around Jodie and closed her eyes, enjoying the weight and smell of her. Jodie had showered first, but she still smelled of soap and her skin was just slightly damp. She pulled the shirt out of her way so she could taste it. Jodie shivered at the touch of her tongue and began tugging at Claire's clothes.

Jodie moved her head down and pressed kisses to Claire's hair, moving until she found her ear. Claire writhed and pulled Jodie closer, lifting her hips to press herself against Jodie's thigh.

"I love you, Claire."

Claire turned her head and kissed Jodie's cheek. Jodie turned her head and their lips found each other in an eager kiss.

There had been a time when she hated being called by her first name. She went by her last name, until that gained an uncomfortable amount of weight. Jodie was only the second person to regularly call her Claire, third if she counted her mother. There were times when it still sounded strange hearing it from other people, but it never felt anything but right coming from Jodie.

"I want you to use your hand on me," Jodie said breathlessly.

"Like this?"

Jodie whimpered and put her head down on Claire's shoulder, murmuring her approval. The bed creaked under them, and Jodie put one hand back against the headboard to keep it steady.

"Love you."

"I love you," Claire said, timing her response so it came mid-orgasm. Jodie nuzzled Claire's neck until she was capable of moving her lips up to suck on a spot she knew to be particularly tender. Claire closed her eyes and took Jodie's hand, put it between her legs, and they worked together with quiet, whispered encouragements until Claire came as well.

Afterward, Jodie settled on top of Claire to catch her breath. Claire held her and, after a few minutes of lying in the dark, moved her hand up to the scruff at the base of Jodie's skull and scratched.

"Hey. You planning to sleep like this?"

"You complaining?" Jodie mumbled. "Got somewhere to be?"

Claire decided she didn't.

She didn't necessarily fall asleep, but she spent close to an hour drifting in and out of wakefulness before her phone rang and woke her completely. Jodie made a noise of disgruntlement and rolled to one side, moving just enough to free Claire and get under the blankets as Claire reached for the chirping monstrosity on the nightstand. The first glance blinded her, and she rubbed her eyes with the back of her hand before she attempted reading the screen again.

"Fruthink uh kay," Jodie asked, the result of trying to ask *everything okay* while her face was buried in the pillow.

"Car accident out by the airport," Claire said. "Fatality."

"Oh no." Jodie was slightly more awake now. She reached up and dragged her fingers down Claire's spine. "Be safe."

Claire turned and bent down to kiss Jodie. "I will. Go back to sleep. I love you."

"I love you."

Claire put her uniform back on. She was the one who usually got these late-night calls, since there was always a chance Randall was taking care of his sick wife. She realized that Rucker had stopped taking them a few years ago because it took him longer to get out of bed and get to wherever he needed to be. The police weren't called out in the middle of the night very often, but it suddenly seemed strange that she was the only officer who could be counted on to show up if something happened after midnight.

As much as she loved Rucker, it was starting to become clearer that maybe it really was time for him to pass the torch.

She looked at the bed to see Jodie was already asleep again. She took a few extra seconds to appreciate the view, reminded herself of the accident's location, and headed out into the night.

***

It was below freezing, and the cruiser's heater took nearly the entire drive to make the car bearable. She was in her heavy jacket and gloves but she was worried she would be shivering when she arrived at the scene. It was technically outside the city limits, but it was still in her jurisdiction. The town fell away quickly, the buildings giving way to the dark of the woods, but soon enough she saw a bloom of light up ahead.

The vehicle was off the road, caught in the crossed beams of two portable lights on tripods. Claire's view of the car was blocked by the fire chief's truck, which she parked behind. Two firefighters stood at the driver-side door. The chief herself, Alexandra Crawford, jogged along the side of the road toward her as she got out of the car.

"Morning, Alex," Claire said.

"Claire, wait." She held out her hands. "We didn't know when we texted. It's Ruck."

Claire's brain was still fogged enough from sleep that she didn't understand. "What's Ruck?"

"The driver," Alex said. "I'm so sorry, Claire, but he didn't make it."

"Didn't..."

She finally looked past Alex and recognized the wreck. It was Ruck's personal vehicle, the front end crushed and still smoking. The windshield was covered with a web of cracks. She could see a body slumped over the steering wheel. His bloody head was turned away toward the passenger side, but she knew Rucker well enough to recognize him.

She tried to rush the scene, but Alex held out her arms and blocked her. Alex was a bit shorter than Claire, but broader in the shoulders and strong enough that trying to get past her would be a waste of effort. Claire rocked back on her feet, completely awake and struggling to keep herself from slipping into shock.

"What... wh-what's the... how..."

"We don't know. We got a 911 call from a hunter who reported a burning car. It had mostly gone out by the time we arrived. It didn't spread very far. It looks like it was contained to the engine. But Claire, he's gone."

"You don't know that, you didn't even take him out of the car..."

"Claire." Alex's grip tightened on her shoulders, keeping her in place. "He was gone when we arrived. There's damage to his head, Claire."

"I just left him."

"I know. Look, there's nothing for you to do here. You shouldn't work the scene. Why don't you just let us take care of it."

She didn't have the energy to fight, so she just nodded. She put her hand on Alex's arm. "Take care of him," she said.

"Absolutely." She twisted and called out to one of the firefighters at the car. The woman jogged over. "Shireen. Can you make sure Claire gets home? You know where she lives?" To Claire, she said, "You're on Argyle, right?"

For a moment, Claire couldn't make sense of the question. "Oh. Yeah, yes. Yeah."

"We'll take care of him," Alex said again. "You just take care of yourself." To Shireen, she said, "Argyle isn't that far from the station. When you drop her off, you can walk over and call it a night. Walt and I can carry on here."

"Yeah, boss," Shireen said.

Shireen put an arm around Claire's shoulders and guided her back to the car. Claire managed to hand over the keys and sleepwalked to the passenger side. She was barely aware they were moving until the bright accident scene rolled away to be replaced by darkness. She closed her eyes and saw the afterimage burned in her mind, like it had been etched there.

"I didn't know him very well," Shireen said. "He seemed... I-I thought he was a good man."

"He was," Claire said quietly.

Shireen didn't say anything else for the rest of the ride. She made sure Claire got into the house okay, returned her keys, and headed out into the night. Claire felt bad about making the woman walk back to the station, even though it was really only a block away, but she wasn't capable of offering any assistance at the moment.

She left the lights off and moved through the house by memory. She went into the kitchen, where the dishes from dinner were waiting to be loaded into the dishwasher. She opened the fridge, uncertain what she was looking for, and finally pushed the door shut to cast the kitchen back into darkness. She turned in a circle and looked around. The moon was shining through the window, and everything in the house looked either blue, black, or gray.

"Claire?" The hall light came on and Jodie appeared. She was still in her nightshirt. "Hon? I thought I heard you leave. Are you already done or is this a dream?"

Claire knew this moment wasn't a dream, and the thought of admitting it was reality finally broke her. She sobbed, then sagged against the counter, stopping herself from a full collapse by pressing her hands flat against the granite. Her arms were trembling. She sobbed again, and this time tears came with the sound.

"God, Claire..." Jodie's arms were suddenly around her. She guided

Claire to the floor, then pulled her closer and began to stroke her hair. "I'm here. I'm right here, baby. What happened?"

Claire had no idea when she would be able to answer that question, so she just cried and let herself be held.

Chapter Two

Jodie managed to get Claire up and led her into the bathroom. She ran the water, undressed Claire, and helped her get in. Claire sank down until the water passed her shoulders and lapped at her neck. Everything was happening in that strange fog of being awake in the middle of the night, when you were confident you weren't creating memories and anything you did would feel like a dream the next day. She lifted her hand out of the water and Jodie gripped it.

"It's really scaring me that you aren't saying anything," Jodie whispered. "You don't have to talk about it, but if you can just say hi..."

Claire opened her eyes and looked into Jodie's concerned eyes. Held in that gaze, with Jodie's hand in hers, she finally felt safe enough to say the words out loud.

"Ruck is gone."

"What? He resigned in the middle of the night?"

Claire shook her head. "He didn't resign. The accident. It was him. He died."

"Oh my god. Claire..." Jodie leaned over the tub and pulled Claire to her for a crushing hug.

"I'm getting your shirt all wet."

"Shh," Jodie whispered. "I'm so sorry you had to see that. Is Randall on the scene?"

Claire shook her head, her face still pressed to Jodie's neck. "Alex. Chief Crawford. The fire department is taking care of it." She sniffled and leaned back. Jodie stroked her hair. "I can't... process it. I just saw him. He was the last person I spoke to, besides you. He can't..." She squeezed her eyes shut.

Jodie cupped her hand in the water and poured it down the back of Claire's neck. It felt fantastic. Claire tried not to think of another night a lifetime ago, another bloody body...

"I know I'm not a cop," Jodie said, "but you said it was an accident."

Claire nodded. "That's what Alex said."

"Well... that's a little weird, isn't it? Your last conversation with him was about taking over as sheriff, and then a few hours later..."

Claire remembered the look on his face when she got into the office. He'd been odd at the park, too. Contemplative.

"Do you think he intentionally..." She furrowed her brow. "I don't think he would do it. Or that he would do it that way. But it still might have been deliberate."

Jodie said, "Murder?"

Claire drew her knees up so they lifted out of the water. "I don't know. I don't want to think about it anymore."

"Do you want me to hold you?"

"Very much."

Jodie got rid of her shirt and briefs, climbed into the tub behind Claire, and wrapped both arms around her. She traced a familiar pattern on Claire's back, the pad of her thumb moving across her shoulder, to an X at the base of her neck, then sweeping down. The scars were long healed, nearly invisible, and covered most of her body. They were the result of her past life, a time she tried not to think about, when a group of men tied her to the back of a car and dragged her through some desert shale. Every time Jodie touched them felt like the pain of that moment was being erased a little more.

"What do you need?"

"This," Claire said. "You."

Jodie held her tighter. Claire hugged her knees and focused on the weight of her wife against her back to shut out everything else in the world.

***

The office was bathed in late afternoon light. Claire, at the time still using a name from another life, waited patiently as her file was examined. She noticed the nameplate on the desk: CALLUM RUCKER. She'd assumed Calvin when she heard the nickname, but she liked this better. It fit the man behind the desk well. He was sitting back in his chair in a casual slump, one hand on his chin with a finger across his lips, as the other held up a tablet computer. Occasionally his thumb would sweep to change the page. He looked like someone's father reading the Sunday paper. Finally he finished reading and put the computer face down on his desktop, pulling his chair forward so he could lean on his elbows.

"Okay." He examined her with eyes as blue as the harbor outside. "That's what you look like on paper. Who are you really?"

"I'm a police officer," Claire said. "That's the long and short of it. Even with everything that happened, I still protected people."

"Went out of your way to do it, seems like. Put yourself in danger more than a couple times. Why?"

Claire didn't have an answer. "What else was I supposed to do?"

Rucker nodded and pressed his lips together. "Yeah. This..." He poked the back of the computer with one finger. "This is a past. We all have a past, Claire. I had a past when I came here. Could have lost everything. Could have ended up being nothing. But they took a chance on me. World like ours, it's pretty damn easy for a white man to get a second chance. Seems like the appropriate thing to do with that is pass it along. You got dealt a rough hand. One of the roughest I've seen in a really long time, honestly. Let me do what I can to help make things easier for you from now on."

He extended a hand across the desk. "Welcome aboard."

Claire smiled and gripped his hand.

***

"No. No, she's asleep right now." A pause. "Yes, I think so, too. I'll see what she says when she wakes up. Okay. Thank you for letting me know."

By the time Jodie ended the call, Claire had rolled onto her back. Jodie looked down at her and smiled sadly. The phone in her hand was Claire's. She reached down and brushed the hair away from Claire's face.

"Hey. You can go back to sleep if you need to. Randall's at the station, and everything's being taken care of. I called and said I might not be in today if you need someone to be with you."

Claire pushed herself up and shook her head. "There are things I need to do. I don't remember getting out of the tub."

"You were practically asleep. I figured you'd be more comfortable here."

"Thank you." She found Jodie's hand, linked their fingers, and pulled it up to kiss her knuckles. Her lips brushed the wedding ring she'd put there four years earlier. "Did you sleep at all?"

"I got the sleep I needed," Jodie said.

"That's not an answer."

Jodie said, "No, but it's what you're getting. I slept next to you." Jodie leaned in and kissed Claire's cheek. "I'll drive you wherever you need to go. Whatever you need me for today, I'm there."

"Okay. Was that Randall on the phone a second ago?"

"No. The mayor wants to see you whenever you're available. She said come by when it's convenient for you and she'll make time."

Claire rubbed her face. "I should probably go by the station first. See how Randall is holding up."

"Your chariot awaits whenever you're ready."

Claire dressed in a clean uniform while Jodie poured coffee into a pair of to-go cups. She couldn't drive the cruiser, so they took Jodie's car into town.

Randall's van was the only vehicle in the station's lot. Inside, they found him at the front desk hunched over his cell phone, typing something into a text message. At the moment his eyes were puffy and red with tears that had either just run dry or were about to overflow.

Randall White was a big man, tall and lanky with just enough muscle to come across as imposing. His blonde hair was cut short on top and shaved on the sides, though Claire knew he'd never served with the military. He had been with the department since long before Claire showed up, and seeing him made her think again about how she seemed to be jumping the line.

"Claire. Hey." He slipped off his chair and went to her, putting one arm around her for a quick squeeze. "Alex told me you were on-site. That must have been terrible."

"Yeah," Claire said. "Where's Minnie?"

"I told her to stay home. She's devastated. I was just texting with some people from her church group to make sure she had someone with her." He looked at Jodie and managed a smile. "Hey, Joe."

She nodded a greeting, staying quiet in acknowledgment that she wasn't part of their work conversation.

"Listen, uh..." He lowered his voice to a conspiratorial whisper. "I'm- I'm not sure, uh... Minnie said Ruck talked to you yesterday, but I don't know if it was about..." His eyes cut toward Rucker's office.

"Yeah, he told me. I'm not sure I accepted. Not sure I have much of a choice now, though."

Randall nodded. "If it helps, you're who I would choose for the job if we had a choice. You're a good cop. We're lucky to have you."

"Thanks," Claire muttered. "Do you have things under control here? I need to go talk with the mayor."

"Yeah, sure. As much as anyone can, anyway. Go on."

She gave his arm a squeeze, thanked him, and headed out again. City Hall was literally across the street from the station, so they walked over. The mayor's office was on the second floor, and Claire could hear the phone ringing as soon as they reached the top of the stairs. Jodie touched Claire's arm to let her know she was hanging back, and Claire nodded as she continued forward.

The mayor's secretary was a man named Connor, and he was in the middle of a conversation with someone on the phone. The door was open behind him and, when he saw Claire coming, he stood and rapped his knuckles twice on the frame without changing his tone. He smiled at Claire, that strange tight expression that didn't convey humor or warmth. It was a near-grimace that said, "I know you're in pain, and I don't know how to deal with that."

The door opened wider and Patricia Hood-Colby stepped out. Claire was always startled by how gorgeous the mayor was. Olive-skinned, chestnut hair, supermodel smile, always perfectly composed. Today she was in a lime-green top and a black skirt, and her hair was pinned up in a tight bun. She looked like the kind of school librarian fantasies were made of.

"Deputy Curran. Claire." She stepped out of her office, taking a few steps forward to escort Claire inside. "I'm so terribly sorry about Cal." She turned to her secretary and made a phone sign with her hand, then cut it to the side. He nodded his understanding and she closed the door. "This is a terrible question to ask, but how are you holding up?"

Claire stood between the two visitor chairs in front of the mayor's desk. "I don't know if there's a right answer to that."

"There is, but no one wants to say 'terrible, barely holding it together.' But in this case, you're absolutely justified." She sat on the edge of her desk. "I know how much he meant to you. He meant a lot to everyone on this island, but you especially. He fought for you. Probably fought harder than you knew."

"Uh-huh." Claire couldn't say more without risking an emotional breakdown.

Patricia gave her a moment before continuing. "I don't know if he had a chance to talk to you about something he'd been considering. It had to do with his eventual retirement."

Claire couldn't help but laugh. "Shit. Was I literally the last person he mentioned it to?"

Patricia smiled. "It's possible. He liked to have his ducks in a row before he pulled the trigger. I admit, I was a little skeptical when he first brought it up. Your history was a little concerning. But he convinced me. And given the circumstances, we don't have much of a choice. I'm surprised Deputy White isn't the one taking over."

"His wife," Claire said. "She's partially paralyzed, and she has appointments with a specialist in Seattle. He needs time off to take her."

"Oh, right. Of course. All the same, I'd like to give you the choice. We need someone to step in as acting sheriff until we have an election. Cal Rucker's recommendation is all I need. The job is yours if you want it."

"Okay," Claire said.

"Okay?"

Claire shrugged. "If it was Ruck's preference, I can fill in until the people have a chance to decide. I think it's better than bringing in some stranger."

"I agree." Patricia nodded and stood up. "I don't think congratulations are appropriate under the circumstances, so I'll just wish you well in the job. I know you'll do Ruck proud."

"I hope you're right."

Patricia offered her hand. "I'll take care of all the official stuff. I want you and Randall and everyone with the department to know we're thinking of them."

"I will. Thank you."

Jodie was waiting outside when Claire left the office. She waited until they were outside, walking back to the car, before she spoke.

"So where to now?"

"I don't know," Claire admitted. "I think I should just go in and... be around for a while. You should go to work."

"Are you sure?"

Claire stopped on the sidewalk and put her hands on Jodie's shoulders. "You've been amazing since last night. But honestly, I need some time to myself to think. And I'm worried about you, too. This has been a lot. If you don't go to work, then go home and get some rest. I don't want you burning out in case tomorrow is even tougher." She kissed Jodie's forehead. "You got me through today, which should have been one of my most difficult days in a long time."

Jodie smiled. "That's why you keep me around."

"Among other reasons." Claire smiled and reached to take Jodie's hands. "Marriage, right? Balance. You got me through the rapids, now I can handle myself for a few hours. And tonight when I get home, I'll reward you for your diligence with a fantastic meal."

"That sounds pretty great actually."

"I thought it might."

Jodie kissed the corner of Claire's mouth. "Call me if you need anything. Even if it's just a quick panic attack or something. You know I'm here for you even when I'm not standing right beside you."

"Always. Now go."

"I love you."

"I love you, too."

They kissed goodbye, and Claire waited until Jodie drove off before she went into the building.

Randall was at his desk and waved her over. "Chief Crawford sent over a bunch of pictures she took of the accident."

Claire braced herself as she crossed the room. Randall got up, partially to give her the seat but more so he could stop looking at the pictures.

The first shot was the entire scene, framed on either side by a dark curtain of trees. Claire grimaced but managed to keep her eyes open. The next shot was closer and had been taken after the engine fire was extinguished. The fire was odd. Cars didn't burst into flames upon wrecking, not like they did in the movies. She would have to ask Jodie what might have caused that. The car door was open, and she got a clear look at

Ruck's bloody collar. She averted her gaze and narrowed her eyes at something in the photo.

"Is there a clear picture of the driver's side door?"

"Yeah, I think so," Randall said from the other side of the desk.

Claire scrolled until she found it. The window was shattered, like the windshield. But it was the pattern that drew her attention.

"Randall, come here." He came around and she pointed. "This didn't break from the impact. Look. The breakage spreads out from this spot." She went back up to the image of the windshield. "The same pattern is here, but it's not as obvious because the windshield shattered when he hit the tree. But you can still see the cracks from the first breakage on the glass that remains."

"Okay," Randall said. "Sorry, I don't see what that means. Ruck's windows were already broken when he wrecked?"

Claire opened his desk drawer and took out a legal pad. She drew a quick sketch of a car. "The break in the driver's side window is here. I think something broke it, then traveled at an angle to the windshield." She drew a dotted line. "We don't know the exact angle, but it had to have been close to this, or else it would've hit him."

"What would've hit him? What do you think it was?"

"A bullet."

***

The car had already been towed, and Claire was grateful for that small mercy. Randall revealed his first task that morning had been to call the funeral home so they could retrieve Ruck's body, and she felt guilty forcing that responsibility on him. Rausch, the mortician, had agreed to preserve the remains until Claire gave the all-clear to begin work. At the time, it felt like the only proper thing to do, but now Claire was grateful nothing had been done, just in case there was evidence of a crime.

Randall drove to the scene. Alex had blocked off one lane with yellow tape, covering the entire area from where the car first went off the road to where it had stopped. Randall got the metal detector from the trunk while Claire walked to the edge of the road. She started at the first tire tracks and walked backward, estimating the speed he might have been going to figure out the arc. When she was facing straight ahead, she motioned Randall over.

"Best guess, he was around here when he suddenly lost control." She held out her arm and marked the angle. "He could have swerved a little before he finally went off-road."

Randall said, "We could go to the car, see if we can figure out an exact angle."

Claire shook her head. "The exit point was destroyed, so the angle would be too wide. It entered the car..." She held up her left hand. "Approximately here. She used her right hand to trace a line, continuing until her arm was fully extended. "We should start the search in that area. If we don't find anything, we move farther up the road."

"Needle in a haystack," Randall said, but he was already walking off the pavement.

"We're not even confident there will be a needle in this haystack."

Randall said, "But it's for Ruck."

"For Ruck," Claire said.

Randall adjusted his grip on the metal detector, started to sweep it, then stopped. He stared at something on the ground, and then held up one hand to motion her over.

"Hey, Claire. C'mere."

"Do you see something?" She walked over to join him.

"I think Ruck's looking out for us." He pointed down. "Careful. Is that...?"

Claire looked where he was pointing. She saw pebbles scattered randomly, various shapes and sizes, most of them obscured by the tall grass. She was about to ask him for a clearer direction to look when she spotted it. Small, gray, oddly-shaped.

"Holy hell," she muttered as she took a baggie out of her pocket. "This might not mean anything. It could be from a hunter."

"That small of a caliber?" Randall said. "This close to a road?"

Claire crouched and used the bag to lift the slug. "It's not unheard of." She closed the bag and held it up to look at it through the plastic. Randall leaned down on the other side of the bag.

"Okay. So let's say this is the little guy who broke through Ruck's driver's side window, then his windshield, and made him crash. Do you think someone actually tried to run him off the road? Are you saying someone was *trying* to kill him?"

"I'm not saying anything yet," Claire said. "But I went looking for a bullet, half-hoping I wouldn't find one, and now... here it is. We didn't have an answer for why Ruck went off the road." She looked up at the sky. It was still overcast. "No snow yet. Definitely no ice."

Randall said, "It was late. He wasn't the youngest guy on the island. He could have drifted off for just a second."

Claire nodded. "A viable theory. It doesn't explain the cracks in the glass, though. And there's another question we need to ask."

"Yeah?"

"Ruck lives on Cedar Point. Over a mile that way." She pointed back toward town. "His house was actually east of the park. But he was driving west, out into the middle of nowhere, in the middle of the night. Where the hell was he going?"

Randall straightened and looked west, as if there was a sign in the distance to reveal the truth. The road continued for about a mile before it curved gently to the south and seemed to vanish into the trees.

"Nothing's out there," he said, "not until you hit the other side of the island."

"Nothing we know of." Claire stood and scanned the ground for any further evidence. "Let's keep looking to see if there's anything else to find."

Randall said, "Claire, if this wasn't just a car accident~"

"I know," she said, cutting him off before he could actually say the words. "I know. Let's just work the scene for now, okay?"

"Yes, ma'am."

***

They spent most of the day at the scene. Randall scoured the ground for any other ammunition, while Claire took her own photos of tire tracks and remains of the wreckage. She also called Rausch and confirmed Rucker hadn't been hit by the bullet. He confirmed there was no evidence of that, but also said there were small shards of safety glass in his neck and lower jaw. It might have happened in the crash, but it also supported her theory of a bullet hitting the window before he went off-road. They finally headed back to town when they'd covered the length of the tire tracks twice over.

"There's never been anything like this since I've been here," Claire said when they were in the car, without clarifying exactly what 'this' entailed.

Randall said, "To be perfectly honest, Claire, me neither. Broken windows, vandalism, theft. A couple of domestic disputes, sure. But this? *Bullets?* Nothing like that. What do we do now?"

"We wait until we have a gun to compare this bullet to," Claire said. "Odds are good it might have been someone fooling around with a gun and things went too far."

He looked over at her. "You actually think that?"

There were too many questions and coincidences. Where had Rucker been going? What was he brooding over in the office? Why had he chosen that day to tell her about his retirement plans? If the shooting was intentional, who in town would have wanted to hurt him?

"No," she admitted. "I don't."

They picked up lunch and took it to the office. Claire ate quickly and then went into Rucker's office. Her office, not that she planned to think of it like that any time soon. She sat behind the desk, turned on the computer, and examined everything laid out in front of her. The mayor was right: he liked to have everything lined up before he moved on something. He didn't do half-measures and he hated walking into a situation unprepared. If he'd been working on something, it would be on his desk or his computer.

The only problem was that she had no idea what it might look like.

"Come on, Ruck," she muttered under her breath. "You couldn't have left a big envelope with my name on it?"

The computer finished booting up and she looked at the desktop. In the center of the screen, just under the logo for the department, was a folder labeled LANCELOT. She smiled and blinked back tears.

"My apologies, Cal."

She clicked on the folder and found a wall of files. Videos, texts, jpgs, all labeled with dates and locations. At the top of the folder was a video file named 0000-Watch Me First. According to the date, it had been saved less than a week ago. She found his headphones in the bottom drawer of the desk and slipped them on. Randall was the only person who might overhear what was about to be said, but she wanted to hear what it was before she shared it with anyone, even him. She clicked on the video and a window popped up.

Ruck was sitting at his desk. It was night, and she assumed he'd filmed it by propping his phone up against a coffee mug. He looked exhausted, but he still smiled and folded his hands on the desk in front of him.

"Hi, Claire," he said.

She bit down on her thumb so she wouldn't cry.

"I don't want to be dramatic, but if you're watching this then you're sitting at my desk going through my files, and that can only mean a couple of things. None of them are very good for me, in the long run." He chuckled softly. "But it means you're the sheriff, and that's good for the town. I completely believe that, and I hope you do, too.

"Something is happening on the island. I'm not entirely sure what it is yet, or who is behind it, but hopefully by the time you're seeing this, I'll have a lot more information saved in this folder. I'm not bringing you or Randall in on this just yet because there's a chance it'll all blow up in my face. If I have to become a sacrificial lamb, I'd rather keep you both safe in the dark."

Claire paused the video and closed her eyes. Had Rucker saved their lives by staying quiet? If he'd brought them in on whatever it was, would the shooter who ran him off the road have come after the two of them as well? She waited until her breathing was steady before she resumed playing.

"Whatever happens, Claire, whether I can't follow through or whatever else, I want you to know I have faith in you. You'll do the right thing and you'll keep the island safe, no matter what that looks like. Just do what you've always done, Claire. That'll be enough."

He reached for the camera and the image froze.

Claire exhaled and leaned back, pulled off her headphones, and stared at the image of Ruck. After a moment, she closed the window and opened the first file.

CHAPTER THREE

RUCKER'S COMPUTER also had his Last Will and Testament, along with details for his funeral. He asked to be cremated, the ashes to be spread by "whoever felt they were up for the job." He had no family, and it seemed he was eager to go out with as little fanfare as possible. Mayor Hood-Colby put together a small ceremony and invited any resident of the island to attend. "Sheriff Callum Rucker dedicated the past three decades to keeping us all safe," she said, quoted in the newspaper. "He deserves a proper memorial."

The weather had grown increasingly cold over the three days since his death. The clouds sank lower and the streets were shrouded in a fog that never seemed to lift. There still hadn't been any snow, but the harbor was starting to look precariously icy in a way that had the ferry captains worried.

Claire woke before dawn the day of Rucker's memorial, showered, and went back to the files she'd printed out from his computer. She sat with them at the dinner table, with only a nearby lamp casting a pale golden glow over the pages. She lost track of time and jumped when the overhead lights came on. She looked up to see Jodie, still in her robe, approaching.

"I know you came to bed, because I cuddled with you for a while. How long have you been up?"

"Not long." She saw the grey light outside that revealed the sun had risen on the other side of the weather. She thumped the papers. "Maybe longer than I thought. I'm still trying to fit all these pieces together. Ruck wasn't exactly a good writer, but you can find the story if you look hard enough. These are months of reports about surveillance. Just watching a group of five or six people who, as far as I can tell, never did anything."

Jodie sat across from her. "Tell me what you've figured out so far."

Claire pushed her hair out of her face and rearranged the papers in front of her like tarot cards.

"A couple of months ago, Ruck became suspicious of some new people in town. At first, they were staying at the Royal House Inn, but after a couple of days they moved out to another place he either never found or never made a note about. But he knew they were still around because he kept seeing them around town. He has pictures of them."

Jodie made a grabbing motion with her hands. Claire found the photos and pushed them across the table.

"He was never able to stop them for anything, not even some minor infraction. It says here he stopped to chat with one of them, just a casual welcome to the island sort of conversation, but the guy just made small talk and then said he was in a hurry."

"So what made him suspicious in the first place? Maybe they're just a group of guys moving to the island. There's nothing illegal about keeping to yourself."

"One of the guys had prison tattoos. He kept them covered up most of the time, but a few of them are hard to hide." She pointed at the picture of one man with the edge of a neck tattoo exposed by his shirt collar. "Guys with prison tattoos, and guys who hang out with those guys, and they all like keeping to themselves...? That's enough to be suspicious."

Jodie said, "Makes sense. These guys are still on the island?"

"As of last week, yes." She shuffled the papers again. "Ruck saw one of them waiting at the ferry lanes. He met someone who drove off the boat, he got in the car, they headed out of town. Going west on Spring Street."

"The same road Rucker was on when he died."

"Yep. He followed them as far as the town limits, but he could tell they'd clocked him. Maybe that's why he was in his personal vehicle that night instead of a squad car."

Jodie ran her tongue over her teeth. "So there were guys in town that Rucker thought were suspicious. They were staying somewhere outside of town, but kept coming back for supplies or to meet people coming in on the ferry. Maybe they were ex-cons who just wanted to lie low. Maybe they didn't like the local cops watching them."

"Maybe," Claire said. "But there has to be more than that. Ruck said something big was coming, and he didn't think he was prepared for when it hit. He must have figured out more than he left here, but where else would be put it? This was his 'If you're watching this, I'm dead' insurance. So why wouldn't he put all his cards on the table?"

"Maybe he didn't want to leave it on the station's computer, for whatever reason. Maybe the information is at his house." She held up a hand to hold off Claire's next comment. "Even if it is, it can wait until after the service. You should probably start getting ready."

Claire sighed. "Yeah. God, I'm not looking forward to this."

Jodie reached across the table and covered Claire's hand with hers. "Just one thing at a time. That's all you have to figure out, okay? And right now, it's the uniform. Your armor, your sword."

Claire chuckled and pushed herself up. "Right. I feel like my hair should be in a braid of some sort."

"I can put your hair in a braid of some sort," Jodie said.

"Thank you." She bent down and kissed the top of Jodie's head. "I love you."

"I love you, too."

As she went to dress, she tried to put her unofficial investigation out of her mind. It might have been nothing, the paranoid obsession of a man who had been a cop for most of his life. But Claire had also been a cop for a long time, and she'd learned not to dismiss gut feelings. Especially not when those feelings were coming from a man like Rucker.

If he smelled smoke, there was bound to be a fire somewhere. It was just a matter of how big it might be.

***

The memorial was held in the public meeting room at Town Hall, and Claire was glad to see the room was fairly packed with people. In the absence of family or a casket, she felt like the proxy center of attention and tried to put on an appropriate face for the people who came up to wish her well or ask how she was doing. For the first time since coming to the island, she felt uncomfortable in her uniform. She'd been acting sheriff for a few days now, but that was all formality. She rarely left the office and no one had actually referred to her by the title until this morning. She kept her arm around Jodie's waist and used her as a life preserver to get her through the sea of people.

Eventually the group was ushered into the main room, and Claire was allowed to take her seat between Randall and Jodie. Randall's wife was also sitting with them, a lovely woman named Jennifer whose wheelchair meant she had to be at the end of the aisle.

When everyone had settled, a petite brunette in a green plaid pantsuit and big librarian glasses stepped onto the stage. She stood at the podium, smoothed down her notes, and smiled at the group. Claire vaguely recognized her, but only knew for sure who it was when she began speaking.

"Hello, everyone, thank you for coming out. Most of you are used to hearing me without seeing my face, so allow me to introduce myself. Most of you know me as Nadine Butler, the voice of KELF Radio. We're here to say goodbye to Sheriff Cal Rucker. I was asked to take part not because I talk for a living, but because of what Mr. Rucker meant to me."

She paused and looked down at the podium, pretending to check her notes. Claire could see she was struggling to control her emotions.

"This island was a very different place not too long ago. I lived most of my life in the closet because I had a job in the public eye, and I was worried about what people might think. I came out by accident, in this very room, with Mr. Rucker standing on this stage. I actually came out *to* him, but everyone else overheard.

"It was as bad as I'd feared. People wanted me fired from my job. I started losing advertisers. People actually protested outside the station demanding my resignation. Cal Rucker stood between me and them. Sometimes literally. And when there was violence, he was the one who made sure I was taken care of. He showed me kindness at a time when it felt like everyone in the world had turned against me. I don't think I ever properly thanked him for that."

Another pause. She looked down at her hands, her lips pressed tightly together.

"At the time, I didn't know how he felt about the fact I was gay. He never said anything one way or another. He just knew I was in danger and did everything in his power to make me feel safe again. So I felt safe whenever I saw him around town after that. I imagine a lot of you probably have stories like that about him, otherwise you wouldn't have come out on such a cold and dreary day. So I'd like to give the opportunity for anyone who has a story to come up here and say a few words about our sheriff."

Alex Crawford was the first to rise. "I limped into this town. I had an injury that, honestly, took way too long to heal. If I want to be completely honest, if someone walked into my station looking the way I did back then, I'd have been really skeptical about hiring her. Sheriff Rucker made a point of coming over and introducing himself the first time he saw me in town. The new firefighter, limping, using a cane. I must have struck a really heroic pose." She smiled. "But he shook my hand. He told me he'd heard good things from my old station, which means he *did* call to check up on me. But I can forgive him for that. He told me to call him any time I needed to talk. I took him up on that more than a few times over the years. He was never too busy to talk. And, uh... I think, I think that's all. Thanks, thank you."

She took her seat.

Next to stand was an elegant older woman with her silver hair pinned back by a large jade clip.

"My name is Vanessa Kavik. Many of you have my work hanging in your office, maybe even your homes. When I first came to the island, I was a bit of a... a nuisance... I had a habit of painting in the nude, and I frequently did it in public. Deputy White is squirming because he used to be the one who had to run me in when people called to complain."

Claire looked to see Randall was indeed blushing.

"I was unrepentant and resistant to being rehabilitated until one day

Sheriff Rucker took me into his office. He asked what he could do to make the island more amenable to my art. He didn't tell me I had to stop painting nude, he asked how we could work together to make sure everyone was satisfied. So we talked and eventually we came to a compromise that we both could live with. And Deputy White hasn't seen me naked for almost five years now."

The room laughed softly.

Vanessa said, "Sheriff Rucker was the sort of man who worked with people to find an answer. He wouldn't insist he knew best, and he wasn't convinced the letter of the law was always the proper route. We were lucky to have him for as long as we did."

Next, the town librarian Cheryl Paxton meekly lifted her hand. Nadine smiled and gestured for her to stand up. Cheryl awkwardly rose, then began to speak at the same time she Signed her words.

"My wife and I were among the first openly lesbian couples on the island. She passed away a little while after Nadine's show. It was still very early, and a lot of attitudes remained closed-minded. But after she passed, Sheriff Rucker came by my house. He spent time with me. He made sure I was being looked after. He was a kind man. He was generous. I'll miss him very, very much."

After Cheryl sat, a few seconds passed with only silence. When it became clear no one else was going to stand, Claire squeezed Jodie's hand, then rose from her seat. Nadine looked at her and smiled.

"How appropriate. Let's bring Acting Sheriff Claire Curran for an official message. Please."

Nadine stepped away from the podium and Claire reluctantly took her place.

"Wow, I wasn't keen on standing at my seat, let alone this. I'm not very big on public speaking. But I'll give it a try for Ruck." She coughed quietly, wishing she'd thought this through. She flexed her fingers on the edge of the podium. "There was a time in my life when I thought I was finished. I didn't see any kind of future. No career, or a place to call home. Even when things changed and I had hope, I didn't think I would ever be lucky enough to have my dream job. Cal took a chance. He saw potential in me, and I've done my best every day for the past six years to make him proud. And I'll keep doing the same thing now that he's entrusted me with filling his shoes."

Her eyes moved to a man with sandy hair leaning against the wall next to the door. He was dressed appropriately in a charcoal suit over a black shirt, but something about him seemed wrong and vaguely obscene. It took her a second to realize it was his expression. He wasn't smirking, but his eyes were narrowed just enough that she felt like he was holding back laughter. He looked like someone who had stepped inside while waiting for the bus and was vaguely amused by what he was witnessing.

"Um." Claire looked away from the man, trying to regain her train of thought. "Cal was a good boss. A great boss. It was an honor to work for him, and I'll do everything in my power to continue his legacy in this town. Thank you."

She stepped away from the podium, trying to look casual and not like she was fleeing. Nadine returned to the podium as Claire retreated into the safety of the audience. Jodie took her hand as soon as she was seated again and leaned in to whisper, "Good job."

She relaxed and rubbed her thumb over Jodie's knuckles. Nadine went on to say that she knew Rucker had several favorite songs and wanted to play a few of them in his honor. While the first song played, Claire looked over her shoulder. The man at the door was still there, but now he wasn't watching the stage.

He was looking directly at her.

She did her best to ignore him during the rest of the music, but she could feel his eyes on her as she thought about the testimonials. Each story had made her feel less and less prepared to take over the job. She was confident in her ability to fulfill the actual duties of the office, but Ruck had gone above and beyond for seemingly every resident of the island. It was daunting to say the least.

When the last song faded, Nadine returned to the podium and thanked everyone for coming.

"Cal requested his ashes be scattered off the western shore, near the lighthouse, but I think we're going to wait for the weather to be a little more agreeable before we do that. Gail's Seafood Shack is having a special luncheon in honor of Sheriff Rucker, and you're all invited to attend that if you don't want to just head home and avoid the weather."

The crowd quickly dispersed after that, but Claire and Jodie remained near the stage because it seemed like everyone wanted a moment with their new sheriff.

"I feel a bit ghoulish," Claire whispered to Jodie between handshakes.

"People just want to know they're in good hands."

"At Ruck's memorial service? It seems a bit..."

"Gauche?"

"I don't use words like that unless I'm doing a crossword."

Jodie chuckled and leaned against Claire's arm. "You're almost through it. Just a little longer and then we'll head to Gail's."

Claire tensed when she saw that the next person to approach was the smirking man in the charcoal suit. He moved like a used car salesman closing in on a sale.

"Deputy... sorry, *Sheriff* Curran." He offered his hand. "I just wanted to take this opportunity to say hello and introduce myself. Dennis Wyman."

Claire took his hand. He immediately clapped his other hand over hers, making her feel as if she'd just been caught in a snare. The smile never left his mouth. Now that he was closer, she could see the smile also never reached his eyes.

"Are you new to the island, Dennis?" she asked.

"Oh, I've been around a little while. A little while. I was hoping we could have a moment to speak in private before this event wrapped up. Just a quick conversation, just the two of us." He turned the smile on Jodie. "No offense."

Jodie said, "Oh, none taken." Claire read the unspoken message in her tone: *The less time spent with you, the better.* "I should probably go say hello to the Warrens anyway."

"Shouldn't we do that together?" Claire asked, locking eyes with her wife. *Don't you dare walk away and leave me with him.*

"I'll make sure they don't leave." *Sorry, babe, you're on your own.*

"Appreciate it." *Divorce.*

Jodie blew Claire a kiss behind Wyman's back, then hurried off into the crowd.

Claire reluctantly gestured for Wyman to lead the way out of the meeting room into a side office. The curtains were drawn, casting deep and gloomy shadows into every corner. All the furniture was child-size, and a bright pastel bookshelf in the corner was full of picture books. She assumed it was some kind of daycare facility. The room was small and freezing. She closed the door behind her but stayed next to it.

"What can I help you with, Mr. Wyman?"

"I'd like to think we can help each other, Sheriff."

Claire said, "I wonder if anything good has ever come from that statement."

He laughed too hard at that, reinforcing her image of a car salesman. "To put it simply, I just want to make sure we have an understanding. A group of friends and I are going to be operating here on the island. We'll be well outside the town limits, completely out of sight and out of mind, nothing you have to worry about. And we would respect your boundaries as well. We'd have to pass through on our way on and off the island, via the ferry, but we wouldn't make any trouble for you, the residents, or any of the lovely tourists who arrive on this shore every day. It would be an entirely symbiotic relationship."

Claire watched him as he spoke, torn between amusement at his audacity and anger at what he was asking.

"Here's the thing, Mr. Wyman. My jurisdiction doesn't end at the edge of town. It covers December Harbor, it goes all the way up to Sholeh Village. My purview is Squire's Isle in its entirety. So if you're telling me of your intention to commit some sort of crime on any square inch of this island, then you and I are going to have a problem."

Wyman didn't drop the smile. He stepped closer and lowered his voice. "I'm telling you, Sheriff Curran, that we don't have to have a problem. Any problem that arises between us will be your doing. I'm just suggesting maybe save yourself some trouble down the road. Maybe save that lovely wife of yours some grief."

Any amusement faded, and Claire was left with rage. "Did you make this same offer to Ruck?"

His expression didn't give anything away. "You never have to see or speak with me again. I can become a ghost to you. Or I can become a... pest. I can tell from your face that you'd prefer the former. You just want me to go away. I'm willing. I want to make it official so neither of us has to worry going forward. You're new to the job. Make it easy on yourself." He held out his hand.

"Easy." Claire smiled now. "You have no idea who you're talking to."

Wyman sighed and dropped his hand, still smiling. She wondered if the wide gleaming grin was permanent.

"Oh, I know who you are," he said, condescension seeping into his voice. "You're Sheriff Claire, the small-town cop with delusions of making a difference."

Claire didn't blink. "Dig deeper."

The tone of her voice finally made his smug grin waver, but he forced it back into place. "Enlighten me."

"I don't think so, Mr. Wyman." She reached back without looking and opened the door, stepping out of his way. "You've taken up enough of a day that's supposed to be dedicated to a better man than you. Why don't you try out that disappearing trick you mentioned earlier?"

He shook his head and chuckled softly. "Sheriff Claire, you surprise me. But I suppose we'll be seeing each other real soon."

"Lance," Claire said.

He stopped and looked back at her. She'd finally thrown him, and she was proud of the confused look that finally wiped the smile off his face.

"Pardon?"

"Claire Lance. That was the name I used before I was married." She closed the office door and stepped around him. "If I find out you or your friends had anything to do with Cal Rucker's death, you're going to find out who I am very fast, Mr. Wyman."

CHAPTER FOUR

CLAIRE CONFIRMED when they got home that Dennis Wyman was one of the men in Rucker's surveillance photos. He seemed to have been around the longest, and was most often seen around the ferry docks. She found one picture with a front-on view of his face and set it aside. That would go up on the wall of her office as soon as she went back in. She checked the database using her laptop and found that Wyman was clean. No wants or warrants out for him in Washington, and he was apparently clear in the rest of the country.

"Good at keeping your nose clean," she muttered.

Jodie had only been home long enough to change into work clothes before she headed out, so Claire was alone in the house. She closed the computer and went to the back door, staring up at the clouds before scanning the small square of grass beyond the porch. She kept hearing her own voice in her head. *Claire Lance.* She hadn't called herself that in four years, since she married Jodie and took her name.

Before that, Lance had been her identity. It was how she thought of herself, how most people referred to her. But it was also a lodestone around her neck. The whole world knew Claire Lance, it seemed. For a while she'd been infamous. There was even a damned song written about her.

In 2008, she was a cop in Chicago, a newly-minted detective on her first undercover assignment. She screwed up, and the group she'd infiltrated learned who she was. They locked her in a room and spent the next few days loading her up with whatever drugs they had on hand. Eventually they let her go, dumped her back in her apartment strung out and craving a fix. What she'd found instead was her girlfriend, Elaine, murdered. She barely had time to process the sight before the police, responding to an anonymous call about screams, broke down the door.

In an instant, Claire's entire life had been shattered. She no longer existed in the world; she was just a ghost watching through a pane of glass at other people who were somehow carrying on with their lives. She escaped custody, she killed the people who set her up, and then she ran. She had no plan or end goal, she just started running.

There were huge chunks of that time she couldn't remember. She had no memory of traveling south to Texas. She remembered days driving through the Rocky Mountains, nights spent in national parks, but specific days were just a blur. Somehow, she ate. Somehow, she earned enough money to put gas in her Mustang. Either that or she stole the gas. It wasn't outside the realm of possibility to think she'd just filled up and drove off.

But there were also days that she remembered with unbelievable clarity. A bar in Texas, the woman who helped startle her back into some semblance of life. She'd seen someone in danger and her instincts took over. She did what she did best: she protected.

She remembered a ranch in Montana, right next to the Canadian border. The first warmhearted sheriff to show her kindness who had found love with a widow, who sparked hope in Claire's chest that maybe she could also find love again.

Mostly she remembered a garage in Washington state, an enraged mechanic storming away from a motorcycle, having just used two fingers to flip off the rider. She remembered the first thing her future wife had ever said to her.

"You can go fuck yourself."

Claire chuckled at the memory. Back then, Jodie had been called Calico. Claire didn't know when or why they stopped using the nickname. It was a good one, worth revisiting.

Jodie was why she settled down, why she had a house and a backyard. It was only right to take her name, because Jodie was the one who truly brought her back to life. But maybe she'd also used the opportunity to hide. Lance was the past, someone she had to be in order to survive. Now she was just Claire, Claire Curran, a police officer on a tiny island in the Pacific Northwest where the worst thing she had to worry about was car thieves and trespassing.

Saying the name to Wyman felt like putting on a mask. It also felt like taking a step back. She had become "modern-day folk hero Claire Lance" as a way to survive. It worked. She survived. This was her reward, what she'd stayed alive to achieve.

She changed out of her uniform and put on her cozy clothes. By the time Jodie got home from work, she was halfway through turning their pantry into a week's worth of meals.

"Honey?" Jodie said cautiously. "I know the forecast is grim, but are you expecting to be buried for the rest of the month?"

"I just needed to clear my head. I didn't even remember the weather. I guess it's good we'll have all this stuff."

Jodie wrapped her arms around Claire and hugged her from behind. "Want to talk about it?"

"You just got home. You've had an insanely long day."

"Just as long as yours." She took Claire's hand, tugging her away from the stove. "Come here. Sit with me on the couch. We can both relax."

Claire turned off the heat and allowed herself to be pulled. Jodie stretched out and motioned for Claire to lay in front of her so they could spoon. Once they were in position, Jodie brushed the hair away from Claire's face and lifted up to kiss her neck.

"There. Now we can both just relax here, and if either of us has anything we want to talk about, the floor is open." She rubbed Claire's shoulder. "I got nothing. You?"

Claire chuckled and reached up to cover Jodie's hand with hers. "It's not your job to be my therapist, you know."

"No. But I like being someone you can count on, trust, and go to for advice. I spend my day working on cars. The people I work with are more comfortable talking to an engine than each other. I crave conversation. Whatever you got, babe, hit me with it. Please, I'm dying here."

Claire sighed and stroked Jodie's fingers. "I called myself Claire Lance today."

"Really? When?"

"With Wyman. That asshole at Rucker's memorial. He's up to something. He's in one of those pictures, and he proposed that I could just look the other way and let him do... whatever the hell it is he's doing. He was trying to intimidate me. He implied I was just some local yokel. It pissed me off, so I told him who I used to be. Just to rattle him."

"I know you went to a lot of trouble to move past that part of your life. No wonder you went on a cooking spree. How did it feel to say the name?"

"Wrong. I'm not that woman anymore. I haven't been her for a long, long time."

Jodie said, "Counterpoint, you *are* that woman, because you'll always be yourself. But you're a more mature, thoughtful version of her. Some people might say that makes you even more dangerous."

Claire made an uncertain noise. "Somehow I don't think so." She rolled onto her back so she could look up at Jodie. "All the things I did when I was on the road... I threw myself into those fights because I had nothing to lose. You didn't know me back then. Not at the start. I could get hit, and it wouldn't even hurt. I would wake up with dried blood on my clothes and no idea when I'd been hurt. A decade ago, I stood on a road next to my car, which had broken down in the middle of nowhere. I just started walking because it didn't matter if I dropped dead before I hit a town.

"But now? I have you. I have a life, and a home, and a career. I have to ask myself if it's worth risking all of that."

Jodie said, "I've seen the scars. I was there when a lot of them were made. I understand being scared to go back to being that person again. But babe, if there's something happening here, something you have the ability to fight, you can't just ignore it. You spent all those years waiting for the chance to be yourself. If you stand aside and do nothing, you'll have failed. You *are* Claire Curran, but you'll always be Claire Lance. The woman who stands up when no one else will. This moment is what you were fighting for."

"I love you, Calico," Claire said.

"Whoa, Calico. There's a blast from the past."

"I'm bringing it back. Your eyes still blow me away."

Jodie smiled and kissed her lips. "I love you, too, my Claire."

Claire drew Jodie's head to her chest and stroked her hair. She could fight, she could stop bad men from doing bad things and hurting other people. She was still Claire Lance. But there was one huge difference this time. When she was on the road, she was only passing through. She was a stranger, a vagabond, a mysterious new arrival with no ties and nothing to anchor her anywhere.

This time she had a home to protect. And she was damn sure not going to let smirking Dennis Wyman sully it without a fight.

***

Claire was surprised to find Randall and Minnie in the office when she arrived. It was almost eleven o'clock on the night of Rucker's memorial, and she'd expected one of the new dispatchers to cover the phones. She and Randall were both on-call if anything needed their attention. Her stomach sank as she realized that order had been hers to make, and she'd dropped the ball.

"Hey, you two, sorry about leaving you stranded up here. You can both head out and I'll take the night shift."

Randall said, "Are you sure? I told Jen I might be here all night."

"Go home. Let her take care of you for a change."

"That actually sounds like a pretty good idea. Thanks, Cl–" He caught himself. "Thanks, boss. I should get used to saying that, I think."

Claire wrinkled her nose. "Whatever you're comfortable with, Randall." He pushed in his chair and left, but Minnie remained at the counter. "You too, Minnie."

"To be honest, if you send me home, I'm just going to be sitting in a comfortable chair and thinking about how sad I am. At least here I'll be useful if the phone rings. Plus I get to keep you company. So I'm happy with staying, if you don't mind."

"You're welcome as long as you want, Minnie."

Claire turned on the light in the briefing room and opened the folder she'd brought with her. She'd chosen the best photos of the men from Rucker's file and lined them up in a row along the top of the whiteboard. She added the only name she had for any of them: Dennis Wyman. The first picture was dated five months earlier, so she estimated they had to have been around for six months to give Ruck time to get suspicious enough to start documenting their behavior.

And that was basically everything she had. It was pitifully little to go on, barely more than a gut feeling. But Dennis Wyman was definitely up to something. He wanted her to look the other way and, when she refused, he made a clear and unmistakable threat. They'd confirmed the bullet that went through Rucker's car window had come from a Glock 9mm, so all she had to do was prove he owned or had access to one to bring him in for questioning.

The phone rang, and she heard the murmur of Minnie's voice as she answered. She went out into the main room to hear the end of the call.

"~Absolutely, yes, ma'am. Okay. We'll have someone right over." She turned in her chair. "Mrs. Vance called to say she's worried about Rose Odell out on Viewpoint Circle. The temperature is going to get down around ten degrees tonight and she doesn't think Rose has a heater in her place. Randall is probably still on the road. I could call and have him swing by for a welfare check."

Claire was already moving to the door. "No, let him go home. I'll check on old Rosie."

"You sure?"

"It's what Ruck would do, right?" Claire took her heavy jacket off the hook and shrugged into it. "I'll keep my ears open. Call me if there's anything else that needs to be done while I'm out."

"Will do, boss."

She was definitely not going to get used to that any time soon. But she knew if Rucker had been there, he would have laughed at her sentimentality. She was the boss, and she wasn't going to be any good to anyone if she pretended otherwise. She also hated the idea of going out into the night to take calls like this, but it was part of the job. In the old days she could have spent all night and every day obsessing over Wyman until she knew the whole story. But now she had a whole island to take care of.

She wouldn't let them down.

***

No one knew Rose Odell's exact age, but it was generally assumed she was well over a century old. Even the oldest residents remembered her being on the island for as long as they could remember. She kept mostly to herself, retired from the flower shop that still bore her name, and it turned out her quaint little home did not have a heater.

She answered the doorbell wearing two sweaters with a quilt wrapped around her shoulders. There was a space heater standing next to her armchair in the living room, but the house was still cold enough to see their breath as Claire convinced her to spend the night somewhere more comfortable. She watched for signs of hypothermia and thankfully didn't see anything worrisome, but she still wasn't going to leave the woman here for the rest of the night.

"Your friend Mrs. Vance was worried about you," Claire said. "She just wants to be sure you have a warm place to sleep tonight. There's a church that's converted some of its study rooms into bedrooms. I called on my way over and the pastor said they have plenty of space for you. If you let me take you, I'll bring you home in the morning and I'll even stop to buy you breakfast."

That finally convinced her to leave. "But Coffee Table Books breakfast. I don't care how long the line is."

"Okay, I promise," Claire said.

She made sure the house was locked tight and led Rose to the car. She kept the quilt around her, and sat in the passenger seat like she was doing Claire a favor. Claire had no problem going along with that if it meant Rose slept in a warm bed tonight.

"Thank you for coming with me," Claire said. "I wouldn't have been able to sleep tonight worrying about you out here."

"Been doing just fine on nights a lot colder than this," Rose muttered. "Your generation is too coddled. Wouldn't last a day. Growing up in the South, we never had heat or air-conditioning. Summers could get up to a hundred-twenty. I bet you wouldn't know what to do in a house that's a hundred-twenty."

Claire smiled at the thought of Rose as a child. "No, ma'am, you'd win that bet. I get grumpy when the temperature goes over eighty, if I'm honest."

Rose sniffed derisively and looked out the window.

"Have you lived on the island long?"

"My whole life," Rose said, as if Claire had accused her of something.

"You just said you grew up in the South..."

"What are you, some kind of detective?"

Claire smirked and kept her eyes on the road.

Rose sighed. "Well, close enough, anyway. My whole second life. Longer than anyone else."

"I believe it."

"Once I got here, I stayed put. Didn't see no reason to wander. I've only gone as far as Seattle as an adult, and as far as I'm concerned, that's as much as I need to see." She sat silently for the rest of the block. At the stop sign, she said, "You're new, though."

"Compared to you, definitely. I've been here about six years. Before this, I lived in Chicago."

Rose snorted as if that confirmed some bias she had. "I don't see the point of big cities. We have everything we need here, *and* the people know one another. Chicago, you had... what, two hundred drug stores and coffee shops. Here we have one place for each. That's all we need!"

"I think you make a very solid point there."

"So why'd you leave?"

Claire said, "Fresh start." She hoped they could leave it at that. She didn't want to get into the fact she'd been living in Chicago on probation, after spending five years as a fugitive for a crime she didn't commit. The fewer people who knew that story the better. Although if she had to campaign for sheriff, the people had a right to know who they were voting for.

She pulled up to the church, where the pastor was waiting at the top of the front steps. He waved and came down to the sidewalk.

"Here you go," she said. "And I won't forget tomorrow. Breakfast. My treat."

"At Coffee Table Books."

Claire said, "Is there anywhere else? Sleep well, Mrs. Odell."

Rose opened the door, twisted to get out of the car, then stopped.

"Rose? Are you all right?"

She twisted back into the car and shut the door. She stared forward. "My wife would be calling me a grumpy old bat right now, and she'd be right. I hate losing arguments to a dead woman." She reached out and fumbled blindly for Claire's hand. Claire met her halfway. The hand felt light as paper, and freezing. "Thank you, Sheriff Curran, for going to all this trouble. It is very much appreciated."

Claire smiled. "You're very welcome, Rosie. Next time it gets this cold, though, you can call us yourself and someone will be happy to drive you somewhere safe. That's the best part about living in a small town, right? We know each other. We take care of each other."

Rose sighed in defeat and nodded. She got out of the car and the pastor came around to help her. He waved to Claire through the windshield and she smiled, returned the wave, and waited until he got Rose inside before she pulled away from the curb. She unhooked the radio mic.

"Minnie, you still there?"

"Nice and cozy, Sheriff. How's Rosie?"

"Set up at the church. I'm going to take a detour through a few neighborhoods to see if I can find anyone else who might need shelter."

"I'll holler if anyone else calls in."

"Appreciate you, Min."

The neighborhood was dark, with every third or fourth house illuminated by security light over the garage or side door. She didn't notice any obvious signs of distress but passed through another neighborhood so she'd be on the road if another call came in. She didn't know what exactly she was looking for. Smoke coming from furnace vents meant that a heater was running, but a lack of smoke didn't necessarily mean the house was unheated. She drove slowly, examined the houses on either side of the street, paying attention to the windows. A lot of the houses had chimneys, and a few were pouring lazy columns of smoke into the night.

She had just decided to take the car back to the station and call it a night when a car pulled up behind her.

Traffic was rarely a problem on the island, even during the height of tourist season, and never this close to midnight. She looked into the rearview but only saw a glare of headlights. They weren't on bright, so she wasn't blinded, but the proximity was sending a clear message.

"You want to go around me, buddy, be my guest."

She pulled to the side of the road. So did her shadow. Her adrenaline spiked and she tightened her grip on the steering wheel. She could get out to confront them, but they would just speed away. License plate would be most likely obscured. She could put the car in reverse and smash into them, but she didn't want to risk damaging either car. There was still a chance there was an innocent explanation.

Their headlights gave them a perfect view of what she was doing. They could see her head and shoulders and probably knew exactly what was going through her mind. Still, they waited.

She rolled down her window and turned off the engine. An immediate wave of cold air washed in through the opening, but she ignored it. The spotlight above her side mirror was controlled by a hand-lever which she gripped and slowly twisted with small enough movements that they weren't given away by her shoulder. It was difficult to find the right angle, but she eventually got it lined up so the lens aimed behind the car and at the driver of her shadow.

She closed her eyes and flicked the light on. She started with one solid beam, shut it off long enough that the driver might have opened his eyes, then flashed it four more times.

The lens was still glowing as she opened the door and climbed out of the car. She walked back to the other vehicle, which remained parked a few feet from the back of her cruiser, and pulled open the driver's side door.

A man she recognized from the photos was behind the wheel, rubbing his eyes with both hands. He twisted and squinted up at her.

"What the hell, bitch?"

"Out of the car," she said.

"Fuck you."

Claire grabbed his arm and hauled him out of the car. "See, I wouldn't have been able to do that if you were wearing a seatbelt." She leaned him against the side of the car. "Add that to following too closely, and I'm sure I can find something about your headlights while I have you sitting in a cell. You have any identification on you?"

"Go to hell."

"The mouth on you," Claire said.

A quick pat-down revealed his pockets were empty, which proved he might not be a total idiot. She took the cuffs from her belt and fastened them on his wrists.

"Okay, until you feel like introducing yourself, I'll just have to call you Grumpy. Let's go." She walked him to the squad car and put him in the backseat. "Sit tight, Grumpy."

She walked back to his car, shut off the engine, and used her flashlight to do a quick search. There were fast food bags spilling out various boxes, old fries, and messy napkins onto the floormats. The closest McDonalds was in Anacortes, which meant he was willing to spend two hours on a ferry to get familiar junk rather than eating on the island. No cell phone, but there was a handgun under the passenger seat.

Paperwork in the glove compartment confirmed the car was a rental, but Wyman's name was the only one listed. At least she had a solid connection between the two men.

She took the keys and the gun, locked the car, and walked back to hers. She got behind the wheel and glanced over her shoulder at Grumpy.

"Last chance, buddy. Want to have a friendly discussion or are we going to spend a night in jail?"

His neck was twisted to look out the window like a petulant child.

"Okay." Claire faced forward. "It'll be nice to have a houseguest."

She pulled away from the curb and headed back to the station. She anticipated a quiet ride, and she was perfectly fine with that. Her passenger, on the other hand, seemed to be uncomfortable with silence.

"You think you got one over on me?"

She drove without answering.

"I could have killed you back then. A couple of times. You were a deer in the headlights. Literally!" He laughed at his own joke, then rocked from side to side. It wasn't comfortable to sit with both hands cuffed behind your back. "All I'd have to have done is get out of the car, pop-pop. Done. 'Cause cops, you guys aren't supposed to shoot first, right? You'd be yelling at me to drop my weapon, but I'd have dropped you before you finished saying it."

Claire said, "Mm-hmm."

"You scared?"

"Of you?" Claire chuckled. "Not particularly. You could have done that, but the fact you didn't meant that you're not calling the shots. There's someone else you're worried about making angry. So instead you sat there with a gun under your seat and a target in your sights and you didn't do anything because you didn't have permission."

"You'll get yours soon enough," he grumbled.

"It does make me wonder if there's a reason you weren't able to do anything. There was no phone in the car, so you didn't call and ask anyone. It makes me think this is a standing order. Maybe because someone went too far already this week and took a shot at another cop." Claire looked at him in the rearview. "Was it you, Grumpy? Did you shoot at my boss?"

He said nothing and rolled his shoulders.

"That's fine. We'll have plenty of time to chat in the next few days."

They were silent for the rest of the ride. She took him in through the back door and went directly to the holding cells. They were technically in a separate building from the rest of the station, and she quickly discovered the heating hadn't been turned on for this space. Their breath plumed in front of their mouths, but she was willing to suffer it until he was processed. Once his gun was safely stowed away, and after she'd taken his picture and entered him into the system, she led him into the center cell.

"Still want to stay quiet, Grumpy?" She held up the sheet of fingerprints she'd just made. "As soon as I enter these into the system, I'll find out your name. I'll give you one more last chance to play nice and just tell me who you are. It could go a long way toward making us friends."

Odds were good she wouldn't get results back for at least three days, but she took a gamble he might not know that. Even a career criminal could be fooled by the instant results cops got on TV shows. Grumpy turned and walked to the bed. He sat down, swung his legs up, and stretched out on top of the blankets.

"All right. Yell if you need anything."

On her way to the main building, she switched on the heat because she wasn't a total monster. But she lowered the thermostat to sixty-five, because he annoyed her.

They had a few people they occasionally used around the office as volunteers and she went through the names in her head. Minnie looked up as she entered.

"Do we still use Harvey Moses?"

Minnie nodded. "He's always eager for a little extra paycheck."

"Call and see if he's willing to pull an all-nighter. We have a guy who needs babysitting."

"Dangerous?" Minnie already had the phone in her hand, dialing with the other.

Claire paused at the door to her office and decided not to share her suspicions about his involvement with Rucker's death.

"Potentially, but nothing too dramatic. I think just having Harvey Moses around will be enough of a deterrent to keep him from trying anything."

Minnie nodded and finished dialing.

Claire went into her office and took off her coat, draping it over the back of her chair. Harvey Moses Ketier was a Samish carpenter who helped out when they needed extra bodies. She didn't doubt she could take Grumpy in a fight, but Harvey Moses was big and imposing enough that Grumpy likely wouldn't even try challenging him.

Minnie appeared in the doorway as Claire was entering the fingerprints into the database. "Harv will be here in about twenty-five minutes. Turns out he was waiting for the call since he figured we'd be shorthanded for a while."

Claire smiled. "He's a good man."

"We're on an island full of 'em," Minnie said.

"Too true. Thank you, Min."

She waved over her shoulder and went back to her desk. She took out her phone and sent a text to Jodie filling her in about the events of the evening. She wouldn't read it until morning, but at least it would be waiting when she woke up. She looked at the time and rubbed her face with both hands before she got up and went to sit with Grumpy until Harvey Moses arrived.

It was going to be a long night.

Chapter Five

HARVEY MOSES Ketier was bulky at the chest and shoulders, the body of someone who earned his size by working with his hands all day. He'd built the nightstands in Claire and Jodie's bedroom, and she had a feeling the majority of houses on Squire's Isle had at least one piece of Ketier's woodworking somewhere in it. His hair was usually worn in a long ponytail that stretched down his back, but tonight it was loose and wild when he knocked on the back door to the holding cells.

Claire let him in and handed him a cup of coffee as he passed over the threshold. He was a whole head taller than her and had to duck to get inside. He accepted the cup with a grateful sigh.

"You're a lifesaver. Thank you."

"You're the lifesaver here," she said. "I can't leave this guy alone, and I think you'd be more imposing than me."

He sipped the coffee reverently. "You want me to play up the big scary Indian role?"

"No, that won't be necessary," Claire said. "Big and male is probably enough to make this guy behave. I would never ask you to play up your ethnicity like that."

Harvey Moses smiled. "No, no, I don't mind it. To me, it's turning a racist's energy back on him. I'm just being me. He's doing all the work to make himself scared."

Claire said, "Be that as it may, I think a little glaring and flexing will be enough."

"You got it. And, um." He tilted his head. "I don't know what to say here. So I'll just say that I think you're going to do a great job and leave it at that.”

“Thanks,” she said, pushing back the emotion threatening to boil up. “Listen, since you brought it up, there’s an open spot on the roster. Have you ever thought about turning pro? Coming on full-time, get the uniform, all the perks...”

Harvey Moses raised an eyebrow. “Huh. Well, not exactly in terms of actually doing anything. Ruck liked to keep the department pretty small, and he already had you and Randall.” He rubbed his chin. “I guess I could start thinking about it realistically...”

“Take your time,” Claire said. “Talk it over with Ramona. I might be making the offer to some other people, so it might be an invitation to apply rather than just handing you the badge. But the work you’ve done with us so far would count in your favor.”

“I’ll keep it in mind.”

She nodded and led him into the holding area. Grumpy was on the edge of his bed, slumped forward with his arms resting on his knees. He looked up when they came in.

“Deputy Ketier, this is Grumpy. Grumpy, this is Deputy Ketier. He’s going to be babysitting you for the rest of the night.”

Grumpy said, “I thought we were getting along so well.”

“Sorry, Grumps, a girl can only spend so much time staring into those baby blues before I start getting all flustered. Play nice, boys. If I get a good report, I might bring you a big breakfast.”

Grumpy waited until she turned to leave before he spoke again. “You worry so much about who I am. Does this guy know who you are?”

Claire stopped.

“We looked you up. Claire Lance. That’s a hell of a story.” To Harvey Moses, he said, “You know that’s her real name?”

“My wife’s ‘real’ name is Fields,” Harvey Moses said conversationally. “Not sure what that has to do with anything.”

“You oughta look her up sometime if you’re working for her. She’s a real badass. She’s a killer. Killed a bunch of folks up in Chicago, then spent a real long time running from the police. She robbed a damn bank!” He laughed. “Whoo, you’re a rock star, Claire Lance! Don’t know how you conned your way into getting a badge, but it makes me feel like this isn’t the most, uh, capable police department.”

Claire looked at Harvey Moses. He was staying stoic and professional, but she could see the confusion in his eyes.

“Have a good night, boys,” she said again.

She left them and went back to the main building. She hoped she’d maintained her composure in the room, but Grumpy had shaken her. She’d dropped her name like a grenade in Wyman’s lap, hoping he would read up on her to know he wasn’t dealing with some yokel. It had been sloppy, and

Grumpy had taken advantage of it.

Claire walked up to Minnie's desk and rested her arms on the edge. Minnie was working on a crossword puzzle but looked up, patient, waiting for Claire to speak first.

"You know who I am, right?"

"I'm not that old, dear. I know who you are, what state we're in, the year..."

Claire smiled. "No. I meant... you know who I really am. Who I was. Before I came to the island. You know my name before I married Jodie."

"Oh! Claire Lance. Of course, dear."

"And you know what that means?"

Minnie leaned back. "I'm not sure what you're asking, hon. I know you had a rough life for a long time. I know you were cleared of some charges and paid your debt for the rest. I assume you did some things you might not be proud of during those years just to get by. Most of all, I know that Callum knew all of this as well. He probably knew more. The man wouldn't have given you a badge if he didn't believe in you. And he wouldn't have given you *that* badge if you hadn't proven yourself worthy."

Claire nodded slowly. "Thank you, Minnie."

"Of course, Sheriff." She looked back down at her crossword. "Do you know who directed a movie called *Taxi Driver?*"

"Scorsese," Claire said, then spelled it.

"Oh, S-E-S-E," Minnie muttered, erasing a mark. "Thank you."

Claire closed the door of her office. There was a map of the island on the wall and she walked over to it. Squire's Isle didn't feel large, but the square mileage made it much bigger than most major cities. The difference was population density. The majority of people lived in December Harbor, with a few people scattered on the north shore in the Village. Everywhere else was wilderness, farms, ranches, and countless wilderness roads that led who-knew-where. Wyman could be hiding anywhere in the island's center and she'd never be able to find him.

He asked her to step back. To ignore whatever he and his cronies were up to. She had no idea what that thing might be except that it had scared Ruck, and it was worth protecting with violence.

Squire's Isle was the first place she'd been able to call home for a very long time. For a while it was Chicago, but the city was grotesquely and forever taken away from her. Even during the year she lived there with Jodie, it had only felt like a waystation until something real came along. Home wasn't where you were forced to sit and wait. Home was safety, security. Home was a place you chose, a place you stayed.

Her home had a cancer in it, and that cancer had just walked up and asked her to ignore it.

Claire went to the window and looked past the row of buildings along

King's Harbor. The security lights and ambient glow from docked boats made it bright enough to see the water, but it looked black as fresh coffee. There was so much royal branding on the island. Squire's Isle, King's Harbor. The local baseball team was the Squire's Knights and the high school even crowned Lords and Ladies for their senior class.

"This is my island," she whispered as if Wyman was somewhere out in the darkness. "Patricia might be the mayor, but I'm the goddamn queen. I'm not letting you spoil this island without a fight."

***

Claire anticipated Wyman would show up bright and early looking for his lost sheep, and he didn't disappoint. She stayed at the station all night, leaving only at six-thirty to fulfill her promise to Rose, getting into Coffee Table Books early before the rush to get a nice, hot breakfast. There was a chance there wouldn't be a rush that morning. The day was uncomfortably frigid, and the ferry only delivered a few paltry vehicles when it finally arrived. Apparently, no one wanted to risk the trip from the mainland under these conditions.

When she got to the church, Claire sat with Rose while she ate her breakfast and talked with her. By the end of their conversation, Rose had reluctantly agreed to stay at the church until the thermostat got above freezing.

She left with a promise she'd come back and have another chat when she had some time. She went back to the station and dealt with the other stubborn senior in her life. Minnie protested that she was absolutely fine and was just starting to get her third wave, and Claire only nodded and escorted her to the back door that led out to the parking lot.

"I know, I'm getting exhausted just watching you," Claire had said. "Please drive carefully. The roads are starting to get icy."

"You better remember this on some long night when I tell *you* to go home and get some rest."

"I promise," Claire sad. "Goodnight, Minnie."

She checked on Harvey Moses to hear a report that there had been no issues during the night. She'd also gotten breakfast for him, along with a smaller plate for Grumpy. The prisoner wasn't awake, and Claire was content to let it get cold rather than wake him up for it.

Five minutes after returning to her desk, Wyman literally darkened the front door of the station. She watched him enter and approach Minnie's desk, craning his neck to look around the empty bullpen.

Claire let him wait for almost a full minute before she stood and left her office. Wyman smiled when he saw her, a smarmy weasel's smile, one that made her dislike of him grow stronger. She had a distinct urge to keep as much distance between them as possible, and she was grateful that the desk was such a barrier. She could only see him from the shoulders up, and the way he rested his hands on the counter made him look like an orphan asking for an extra helping of gruel.

"Good morning, Mr. Wyman," Claire said.

"Sheriff Claire Lance," he said. "I believe you're holding onto an associate of mine. I'd like to get him back. I'm prepared to pay bail."

Claire twisted to look back toward the holding cells. "Do I...?"

"Got a lot of folks back there?" Wyman asked with a chuckle. "George Lile."

"Oh, right, him." At least now she had a proper name for Grumpy. "Unfortunately he hasn't been arraigned yet. There's no bail to be paid."

Wyman's shoulders slumped. "Uh-huh. Well, when do you expect that might happen?"

"It could be a little while. We share a judge with the rest of the archipelago, and right now she's on Lucas Island. The way the weather is, we might be waiting days for her to get over here."

Wyman let his mask slip a little, and his smile looked pained. "You can't hold him indefinitely."

"No," Claire admitted. "But long enough. He had a weapon in his car. He threatened a police officer."

"He..." Wyman bit down on whatever he was about to say, swung his head to the side, and tried to get back on script. "Well. I understand that circumstances are less than ideal. Can I at least have a word with him?"

"Sure you can, absolutely."

She motioned him to come around the desk and pointed for him to lead the way. She fell into step behind him. He looked over his shoulder.

"I don't know what you're trying to achieve here."

"I'm doing my job, Mr. Wyman."

He chuckled. "Sure. Sure. But it seems to me like you're making your job a hell of a lot harder than it has to be." He opened the door to the holding cells and looked at her. He held out one hand. "Just shake my hand, we make our little agreement, it's win-win. You never see me or mine again."

"As appealing as that sounds," Claire said, "your friend is just at the end of this hallway."

Wyman sighed and stepped into the hall. Claire followed. For the next few seconds, until they reached the other door, they were completely alone and cut off. No security cameras, no windows, no one to overhear them. She stared at the back of his head and let the question come out.

"Did George kill Sheriff Rucker?"

She actually saw his shoulders move as he flinched. He turned slowly to face her. "I don't know what you're talking about."

"It's just you and me now, Dennis." She kept her voice low and met his gaze without blinking.

He returned the stare. "I don't know what you're talking about,

Sheriff."

He turned back around and opened the door. Claire reached past him and pushed the door shut again, leaving her hand flat on the door and her arm extended over Wyman's shoulder.

"You know who I am. What I've done. If I find out you or any of your people had anything to do with him dying... and I mean *anything*... I'm going to make sure you pay for it."

Wyman remained still. "Why, that almost sounded like a threat. I have half a mind to go report it to the mayor."

"You're welcome to do that, Dennis. But that would involve explaining who you are and what you're doing on the island. I get the impression you'd rather avoid that at all costs."

Wyman didn't move. He kept his hand on the knob. Claire kept her hand on the door.

He sighed. "I didn't tell anyone to hurt Mr. Rucker in any way, shape, or form. I'd be more than happy to ask George personally if you'd let me continue through this door."

She left her hand in place for another beat, then dropped it and took a step back. He opened the door and stepped through. Harvey Moses was watching them.

"Everything okay, Sheriff?"

"Fine, Deputy Ketier." She stopped a respectable distance behind Wyman. Harvey Moses would know she'd used the title to make him appear more official than he actually was. He sat up straighter in his chair and crossed his arms over his chest. George got up off the bed and walked to the bars.

Wyman looked at Claire. "May I speak privately with my friend?"

Harvey Moses said, "You ain't his lawyer."

Wyman grimaced at him and faced George. "How are you doing, pal? Looks like you got yourself in a little bit of a pickle."

"I don't know what this bitch's problem~"

"Sh, sh, sh," Wyman scolded. "Let's not start that up, okay."

George grunted. "You here to bail me out?"

"They haven't set bail. They said it could take a while." He glared over his shoulder at Claire. "In the meantime, do you need anything?"

"I'm good. I can stay here as long as I need. Comfy bed, decent food."

Wyman nodded. "Keep strong. And keep track of any of the shit they pull. Bring it up in front of the judge, could help get you out of here."

George nodded and then shot a look of pure hatred at Claire.

She winked at him.

Wyman said, "Stay strong, George. You won't be in there long, I promise."

Claire gestured at the door and Wyman once again led her into the dark hallway. This time they passed to the other building in silence until Wyman was almost to the exit.

"Have a nice day, Mr. Wyman," she said.

He flicked his hand dismissively over his shoulder. She watched him go and noticed snow had started to fall while they'd been in the back. The flakes were tumbling very gently and, when she got closer to look out the window, she saw there was just the thinnest layer of white powder on the streets and sidewalks. Wyman left clear footprints as he walked down the front path and got into a red Chevy Tahoe. She went to her office, grabbed her jacket, and went back to the cells.

"Hold down the fort for me, Harvey Moses," she said. "Randall should be here before too long. If anyone calls before he arrives, shout at me on the radio."

"Sure thing. Where you heading?"

"Patrol," Claire said.

***

She left four minutes after Wyman. The streets downtown were already crosshatched with tire marks, which were in turn already starting to get wiped out by new snowfall, but she had a pretty good idea where Wyman was heading. She drove to the scene of Rucker's accident, keeping an eye out for the red Tahoe as she went through town. The road was traveled rarely enough that she suspected no one would be randomly using it today. Sure enough, when she reached the site of the accident, there was only one pair of tracks in the fresh snow. It was wide enough for a Tahoe, which was enough proof for her to follow to see where they led.

The cruiser had a GPS which recorded everywhere she traveled, and she checked to make sure it was on. She slowed down so she wouldn't round a corner and wind up right behind Wyman, but she was confident he had enough of a head start that he would reach his destination long before she did.

It was surprising how quickly the road transitioned from town, to open farmland, to spooky woods with trees crowding in on either side of the road. The woods weren't actually as thick and foreboding as they seemed. Usually there was only one or two rows of trees and maybe a sharp incline before she was back in wide open spaces.

The interior woods also concealed private land, homes on small tracks of land, accessible only by narrow winding roads peppered with NO TRESPASSING and PRIVATE PROPERTY signs. Most of these roads were identified by homemade markers with the name of the current resident or inside jokes. She passed Lois Lane, Schofield Drive, and Spence Alley before the tracks veered right onto a dirt road with no marker.

Claire slowed enough to look up the road, which disappeared after a single sharp turn. A row of rusted mailboxes were nailed to a wooden plank, indicating there were at least six residences on the road. She made a note on the GPS and accelerated past, taking the long way back to town. She drove directly to the post office and parked in front of the main entrance. The whole lot was empty and quickly becoming blanketed with snow.

She downloaded the GPS information to her phone and took it inside, a warm cave of soft orange light. The main room had two full walls with row upon row of small metal PO boxes that shined as if they had just been polished. The wall opposite the entrance was taken up by a long counter with a single window that looked into a back room full of sorting machines and large rolling carts.

Claire approached the desk and rang the bell. A minute passed, then two, and she had her hand poised to ring the bell again when she heard a chipper voice coming from the far back.

"I'm coming! Just a sec!"

She waited and, as promised, a young woman came strolling out of the back room. She was petite, but walked with her head high and shoulders back like she could dominate any room she entered. She smiled, breathless, and fast-walked up to the counter. She wore the standard light blue uniform blouse and navy uniform trousers, but she managed to make it look like an outfit she had just thrown together. Her nametag identified her as Roni.

"So sorry, Sheriff. It's just me today. I guess that whole rain, snow, sleet thing is more of a guideline for some people, huh?" She used the back of her hand to sweep a thick wing of black hair out of her face. "What can I do for you?"

"I'm hoping you can do something for me," Claire said. "It might not be totally legal."

"Ooh, I'm intrigued." Roni rested her elbows on the counter and leaned in, raising an eyebrow. "Why don't you shoot me a hypothetical and I'll tell you what I can do for you?"

Claire showed her the phone. "Can you tell me who lives on this road? There's no marker, but it's just east of Spence Alley on Border Road."

Roni's face fell. "Oh. That's easy, and I don't think I'm breaking any rules telling you there's nobody. We don't deliver anything there."

"Are you sure?"

"Spence Alley is the end of that route, and even that doesn't have anything ninety percent of the time. There are six old houses on the road, and the mailboxes are obviously still there, but no one's lived in any of those places for at least as long as I've been working here. Wish I could have been more help."

Claire put the phone back in her pocket and stepped back from the counter. "You've been a lot of help, actually. Thank you."

"Any time, Sheriff. Maybe next time I can actually bend a few rules for you."

"I wouldn't want to get you in trouble."

"Sometimes trouble is worth it."

Claire hesitated, uncertain if she was being flirted with. She smiled, dipped her chin once, and turned to leave. When she looked back, Roni was still watching her. The postmistress smiled, showing her teeth, and waved her fingers. Claire waved back and headed out into the snow.

The conversation had been more helpful than Roni thought. Now she knew that Wyman had driven to one of six abandoned houses out in the middle of nowhere. They must have been pretty run-down and primitive, but she doubted it would take much effort to make them habitable. She would have to find a way to get a look without attracting attention.

Back in the car, she picked up the radio microphone. "This is Sheriff Curran. Anyone back home listening?"

A second later, Randall's voice came through the speaker. "Copy, Sheriff. I heard you had a pretty wild night last night."

"Nowhere near my wildest," she said. "Is our guest behaving himself?"

"Yeah, he's being a good boy. No calls so far. What are you up to now?"

"Fishing, mostly." Claire watched snow accumulate on the windshield. "I was thinking about a detour to Ruck's house. Maybe I can find something he didn't want at the office or on any official computer."

"Good thinking. If you don't happen to have a key~"

Claire smiled. "Back yard, under the third log in the woodpile. Stupid."

Randall laughed. "I tried to talk him out of keeping it there at least a dozen times. I told him it would be pretty embarrassing if anyone found out the sheriff got his house robbed by someone using a key he left in the yard."

Claire adopted a gruff, male voice. "Yeah, well, that's about *half* as humiliating than having my next-door neighbor crawl in my side window 'cause I locked myself out again."

Randall laughed again. "Good luck, Sheriff."

"Thanks. I'll check in when I'm on the way back. Call me if anything comes up."

She hung up the microphone and left the post office.

On the drive to Rucker's house, she got a pretty good idea why there hadn't been any calls all morning; the island was hibernating. Most of the businesses she passed were open, but none of them seemed to have customers. Coffee Table Books was more abandoned than she'd ever seen it, and the streets were wide open.

The houses on Rucker's street had battened down the hatches. Smoke rose lazily from chimneys and windows glowed cozily as she passed. A few children bundled up in several layers of winter gear conspired on lawns in anticipation of snowball battles and building snowmen. Claire waved to them as she passed, but her good mood faded as she pulled into Rucker's driveway. A tall brick mailbox stood at the curb, the edges glassy with ice except for an area around the front slot which had been opened by mailmen. The mail could be accessed by opening a hatch on the back of the brick column, which was still encased with ice.

Claire listened to the engine idle and stared at the dark windows of the house for a long time. It already felt abandoned, left behind, like the last remnant of a man she'd cared deeply for. He'd been such a part of the island, and now he was just gone. It didn't seem right. Finally she turned off the car and got out.

As expected, under the log she found a metal ring with three keys on it. She took it to the back door and let herself in. She'd been to his house a few times, for beers and dinners, random get-togethers. It was a typical bachelor pad. Messy kitchen, but not horribly so, and an extremely male-centric front room: dark colors, a leather chair, a large TV. He had a well-stocked bookshelf which was filled with paperbacks and biographies of men in cowboy hats Claire didn't recognize. She and Jodie had an open invitation to come over for dinner or watch a movie. Claire usually only accepted if Jodie was out doing something with her friends from the garage. She assumed if she was feeling lonely, Rucker probably was, too.

The house was absolutely freezing, so her first stop was the thermostat. Fortunately, the electricity was still on and the furnace began quietly humming as soon as she flipped the switch.

Shivering, Claire continued down the hallway to the front bedroom which had been converted into an office. She turned on the light and, as usual, her eye was drawn to the photo hanging between the two windows. It showed a much younger Callum Rucker, with thinning black hair and an ill-advised Clark Gable mustache with his arms around a beautiful brunette and a young boy. Rucker was smiling bigger in the picture than she'd ever seen in real life. He smiled, he laughed, but he kept his lips pressed together as if the act of smiling caused him pain.

"*They died,*" Rucker told her one night, unprompted. They were both two beers in, watching the Mariners on his TV. Claire didn't say anything but watched him attentively. "*Murdered. Someone I arrested but couldn't keep in jail. He came after me. Killed them both. So I found him. And I killed him.*"

Claire had felt cold at the admission, handed over like he was commenting on the game. His eyes had been on the screen but after a moment he looked at her.

"*That's why I gave you a second chance. Because this island was my second chance. I hope it's as good for you as it's been for me.*"

They touched the necks of their bottles together and went back to the game. Rucker never mentioned it again but Claire had done some research on her own. Rucker's department knew what he'd done, of course they did, but the investigating officers agreed to look the other way rather than arrest him for what they considered justice. But in return, he had to walk away.

From the job, from his town, everything. It had probably been a small sacrifice. Without the people who made it a home, one city was the same as another.

She sat at the desk and smelled Rucker's cologne, his aftershave, and resisted the urge to look over her shoulder to see if he'd entered the room behind her.

The desktop was tidy, and the drawers were neatly arranged with each file catalogued. She chose one folder at random and saw crime statistics for Squire's Isle from 2004-2005. Packages stolen from front porches, citizen assists, traffic stops, and welfare checks. It was still standard stuff fifteen years later. She put the folder back and moved ahead until she reached the current year. Tucked in among the normal files was a small notebook.

Claire tried not to get excited as she took it out and opened it to the front page, where he'd written a list of names. Rucker's handwriting was as neat and tidy as everything else in his house, and the slanted letters were easy to read. Only two of the names meant anything to her: Dennis Wyman and George Lile. Wyman's name was fourth on the list but circled enough times that Claire knew Rucker had identified him as the leader.

Two or three pages of the notebook were dedicated to each name, though some had much more information than others. It looked like general biographical information, the sort of things anyone could get without access to a police database, but it would save her a lot of legwork.

She closed the book and put it aside to take it with her when she left. The notebook would be handy, but so far it seemed like it was only the most basic of information. She'd seen the work he'd done on the case, but nothing about what piqued his interest in the first place. Something big enough to make him want to retire. Something he wanted her to be in charge of handling.

"Come on, Cal," she muttered as she scanned the room. "Something scared you. It had to be more than a bunch of unfriendly guys hanging around the ferry lanes. So what did you find out?"

Claire went back through the house, this time looking for less obvious hiding places. She tried to think like Ruck. Where would she have hidden something important if she lived in this house? If she suspected Wyman or one of his goons might break in here and look for it? Ruck was the kind of guy who hid his key under a log in his yard, but he could be surprisingly sly when absolutely necessary.

There were the obvious places - the chimney, the toilet tank, the crisper drawer in the fridge - but she checked them anyway and came up empty. She had to entertain the possibility Wyman had already been there, but she'd seen no signs of a break-in and Rucker's address wasn't listed anywhere publicly. Of course, she had just proven the woman at the post office was willing to bend the rules under the right circumstances. If someone~

She stopped in the middle of running her hand along the underside of the couch and followed that train of thought. When the realization clicked, she pushed up off the floor and went to the front door. Rucker had put everything in order before heading down the road that night. He talked to Mayor Hood-Colby and Randall about who should take over for him. He couldn't have known he would die that night, but he'd certainly planned for the possibility.

The snow was thick enough to crunch under her shoes as she walked across the lawn. He wouldn't have left vital evidence lying around the house waiting to be discovered by whoever he'd been on the way to confront. She took his keys from her pocket and thumbed the smallest one. She hadn't given much thought to what it might open. Subconsciously, she'd assumed a gun safe or something similar. But now she knew exactly what it opened.

She crouched behind the brick pillar of the mailbox and used her truncheon to break the ice on the access hatch. The key fit perfectly and the door squeaked when she opened it. A small pile of envelopes, flyers, and one large padded envelope. She ignored the regular mail and took out the envelope.

The address was written in Rucker's handwriting, with the station as its return address. She ripped it open and looked inside to find a flash drive and a sheet of paper. She took out the paper and unfolded it to see three words written in black Sharpie. She pressed her fingers against her eyes, worried the tears would freeze to her face if she let them fall. The message was simple.

"GOOD JOB, CLAIRE."

CHAPTER SIX

THE FLASH drive sat on the coffee table while Claire cooked dinner, and remained there after Jodie came home. They ate together on the couch with the flash drive sitting in a ceramic bowl between their propped-up feet. Claire stared at it as she explained to Jodie everything she'd discovered over the past day.

"So why don't you plug it into a computer and see what it is?" Jodie asked when she finished.

"It's been sitting in a freezing mailbox for days," Claire said. "It needs to… I don't know, thaw out or acclimate to room temperature or something before it works right."

Jodie furrowed her brow. "Is that true?"

"I don't know," Claire admitted. She used the bottom of her beer bottle to make a circle on the arm of the couch. "Ruck died for whatever is on that flash drive. But whatever is on that flash drive killed him. Wyman is clearly a piece of shit, so I want to do whatever I can to get him off the island. But at the same time…" She shook her head. "What if I'm okay with ignoring whatever it is? What if I decide it's not worth the risk? I'll have to live with knowing I chose myself over… drugs? Guns? Whatever the hell Wyman has brewing out there. The longer I put off learning what it is, the longer I can live without knowing if there's a line I'm willing to cross."

"You can take as long as you want, Claire. But I think we both know which side of that line you'll land on."

Claire took Jodie's hand, linking their fingers together. They sat silently for a few seconds.

"So…" Jodie's lips twisted into a wry smile. "Tell me more about this mailwoman who was flirting with you."

"She wasn't~"

Jodie laughed and leaned back. "Of *course* she was flirting with you!"

"She couldn't have been thirty years old," Claire countered.

"So?"

"I'm a few years older than thirty."

Jodie narrowed her eyes in playful suspicion. "So am I. Are you implying that makes someone less attractive?"

"Absolutely not, my love. But people that age tend to be a little blind to true beauty. She wasn't flirting with me. It was the uniform."

"She wasn't trying to get out of a ticket, babe." She toyed with Claire's collar. "Although I do admit, the uniform is quite fetching."

Claire rubbed the jumpsuit over Jodie's thigh. "I'm pretty fond of yours as well."

Jodie leaned in and kissed Claire's lips. "Would it be easier for you if I was here when you looked at the file, or would you rather be alone?"

"I think I have to be alone. But thank you for the offer."

"I'll be in the bedroom if you change your mind." She stood up and slipped her hand out of Claire's.

Claire looked up, almost panicked. "What, now...?"

Jodie bent down and cupped Claire's face. "Yes, Claire. Now." She pecked Claire's lips. "Whatever you find on there, we'll deal with it together. But you need to get through it. The longer you wait, the harder it'll be."

"All right. You're right. Of course you're right."

"Call if it's too much."

Claire watched her go, then looked at the flash drive. She sighed and got up, snatched the drive off the table, and went to the laptop they mostly used for Netflix and email. She figured out how to plug the device into the side, sat down at the dinner table with the screen angled toward the wall. She didn't think anyone would peek in the windows, but she figured a little paranoia would be good until she had some idea of what she would be dealing with.

She found files separated into folders that were labeled with the names from Rucker's notebook. She chose George's, clicked on a jpg at random, and found herself looking at George Lile sitting at a table outside Gail's. It looked like it was taken in the summer. His posture was slightly hunched forward, as if he expected to get up and leave at any second and wanted to be ready. He was looking in the direction of the ferry, eyes narrowed against the sun.

"Come on, Ruck, why are you taking pictures of all these guys? They're never doing anything." She scanned the table behind him and the wooden flooring by his feet to see if he had a baggy of drugs he intended to hand off. Nothing. He could have been any random tourist or resident waiting for a friend to arrive, if not for the anxious energy that was apparent even in a still photograph. There was absolutely nothing in the image to pique the interest of~

Then it clicked.

She opened a few more images, her skin getting cold as the remnants of her dinner soured in her stomach. She clicked through the folders and saw the other men from Rucker's hit list across several months, all of them at or near the ferry lanes. It was like one of those Magic Eye posters; once she realized what she was looking for, she couldn't help but see it.

Jodie came out of the bedroom sometime later. She was dressed for bed in a long T-shirt, and she slowed on her way to the kitchen. Claire was seated at the table, her uniform blouse off so she was wearing the white V-neck undershirt. The computer was on but her face was turned toward the window instead of the screen. She didn't know how long it had been since she stopped opening images, but it must have been at least ten minutes.

"Honey? Are you okay?"

Claire shook her head. She didn't trust herself to speak. Jodie came over and crouched next to her chair.

"Bad?"

Claire nodded.

"Tell me."

Claire looked at the computer. She swept her finger across the track pad, clicked, and an image appeared on the screen. Jodie looked at it.

"Okay," she said. "That's one of the men, isn't it?"

Claire clicked on another image without saying anything. It showed the same man, but this was a different day going by his outfit. Another picture, another day. She watched Jodie, who scanned each photo with growing confusion.

"He's not doing anything, babe."

"Ruck saw something that made him take the picture." Claire's voice was strained. She clicked back through the pictures she'd opened. "Do you see anything that might make a sheriff take a photo of someone at the ferry lanes?"

Jodie shook her head. "I'm sorry. I~ wait." She sat up straighter, standing on her knees instead of kneeling, and leaned closer to the screen. She pointed at a teenage girl sitting on a bench at the edge of the frame. "Is that girl with him...? Go back to the picture of him walking in front of the ticket office." Claire opened it. "There's another girl right there."

Claire nodded, furious with herself for not seeing it before. The men were rarely centered in the shot, but off-center or askew. Claire thought it was due to the fact they were usually in motion when the pictures were taken, but now she could see the truth. Rucker had framed the shots perfectly to include girls who were walking behind the men, or seated near them.

Jodie backed away from the table. "What is that, Claire?"

"You know," Claire said.

"No," Jodie said. "No, it's not... no."

Claire pushed the computer so the screen wasn't aimed directly at her.

"Wyman is the middleman," Claire said. "That was in Ruck's notebook. He had the basics figured out, or at least a pretty solid theory. The women come in on boats from who knows where. Maybe Canada. They could start in the Pacific and come down the Salish Sea. They arrive somewhere on the island... I also don't know where. Ruck hadn't figured that out yet, but he was trying to find it. I think if the assholes were smart, they would use different places every time."

Jodie had filled a glass with water, but she just stared down into it as she leaned against the counter and listened silently.

"Wyman or one of his goons picks them up. Take them to the six abandoned houses. Then hold them there until... I don't know, until they have someplace to take them."

"Until someone buys them," Jodie said. "Say what it is."

"Yeah," Claire said softly.

Jodie came back to the table. "How could Cal just let this happen? I mean, fuck!" She slapped the table next to the laptop. "Just go in and burn the fucking place down!"

Claire stood up and put her arms around Jodie. "It's not that simple."

"I don't care about court or any of that shit." Jodie still sounded enraged, but she folded herself into Claire's embrace and accepted the hug. "They're holding women prisoner, Claire. They could be out there right now."

"I know. But if I run in there guns blazing, we have no idea what Wyman will do. They could just kill the women they're holding. The only bright side to this is the weather. The ferries are on reduced service, and I highly doubt whoever is bringing the women in will risk transporting them when the water is half ice. They're not going to get anyone else for a while, and whoever they have now will stay on the island until the thaw."

The anger had faded out of Jodie's voice when she spoke again, leaving only fear. "Get them, Claire. Please."

Claire didn't know if she meant get the bad guys, or save the women, but either way she nodded. "I will, Joe. I will."

***

It was easy getting Jodie back to bed, not so easy convincing her to stay there alone.

"You're not going out there tonight. I know what I said, but... no, please. I don't believe in bad omens, but Rucker~"

"I'm not going out there," Claire promised. "The place is in the middle of nowhere, so I'd have to use my headlights just to keep from ending up in a ditch. I'm not about to walk into a place I've never even seen with my car lit up like Christmas. But there's something I have to do. I promise I'll be safe." She smoothed down the blanket over Jodie's stomach as if she was tucking her in, then kissed her lips. "I'll be a phone call away if you need to hear my voice."

"I love you, Claire."

"I love you, too. Try to get some sleep."

Jodie nodded. When Claire reached for the lamp, Jodie said, "Leave it on? Just for tonight. Since you won't be here."

"Yeah. Okay."

She reluctantly put her uniform back on. As she was about to leave the bedroom, Jodie stopped her.

"Where's your hat?"

"I don't have a hat."

"The Smokey the Bear hat."

Claire smiled. "That was Ruck's. I wouldn't feel right wearing it even if they'd given it to me."

"Sheriff should wear a hat."

"I don't have~" Claire stopped herself. "Seriously?"

Jodie smiled and lifted a shoulder in a shrug. "It's part of your armor."

Claire sighed, shook her head, and went to the closet. She took out the black Stetson and placed it on her head. She looked back at the bed and held her hands out to either side.

"Better?"

"Much better. Go take care of business, Deputy Curran."

Claire touched the brim of her hat. "Yes, ma'am."

***

Randall was at the front desk when Claire showed up. He smiled when he saw the hat, but his forehead was creased with confusion. "Boss? What are you doing here?"

"I need to have a conversation with the prisoner."

"Have you even slept today?"

Claire tried to remember. She was sure she'd closed her eyes for a few minutes after dinner. It didn't matter.

"I'll get some sleep in a bit." She let herself into the bullpen and headed across the office. "Anything I need to know?"

Randall slipped off his chair and followed her. "Minnie came in for a little while this afternoon. Harvey Moses headed home not long after. I called a couple of our other volunteers, and none of them seemed very confident about coming out in these conditions. Same with the dispatchers. So I thought I'd hunker down for the long haul. I got Jennifer's Kindle, and some puzzle books, and I brought a whole thing of soups, so I'm pretty much all set."

"Good. Thanks, Randall."

He cleared his throat. "Uh, like I said, boss, I told Jennifer I'd be pulling the night shift, so I'm really not sure what you're doing here."

"Uh-huh. Calls?"

Randall twisted his lips, annoyed at being ignored. "Well, we had a minor car accident outside the general store but that was it. No one's going out in this weather. Well, no one sane."

"Is that a crack at my sanity, Deputy?" Claire said without looking back at him. "I am your superior officer."

"Does that mean you'll stop stealing my lunch from the fridge?"

"Tell your wife to stop making those chicken sandwiches and maybe it'll be safe."

She held up her hand before they entered the holding cells so he'd know the bantering was over. "Wait here."

"You sure?"

"Yeah."

He put a hand on her arm and lowered his voice. "Randall and Claire time right now. No badges or titles. What are you doing here?"

Claire thought about keeping him in the dark, but decided he'd earned her trust. "I'm dealing with something that's going to take a lot of my time. This is why Ruck wanted me in charge. You'll have to cover my butt here with the day-to-day stuff until I'm finished."

"Ten-four, Sheriff," he said.

He dropped his hand, staying in the hall as she opened the door and stepped into the cold back room. George was lying on his cot and barely lifted his head at the sound of her arrival. She walked up to the bars and stared at him.

"Get up."

"I'm comfortable."

"Get on your fucking feet."

That got his attention. He lifted his head and stared at her long enough that she thought he'd refuse again. Finally he swung his feet over the edge of the cot and pushed himself up. He moved slowly, like an old man whose joints had gone rusty in the cold. He strolled up to the bars and held his hands out to either side.

"What happened to civility?"

"I gave you a chance to tell me your name. You didn't take advantage of it. So I'm going to give you one more way out. We already have you, so you have an opportunity your friends don't. You can talk. You can be cooperative, tell us what we need to know so we can put a stop to this. It might help you in the long run. Maybe get you a shorter sentence."

George smirked. "Doesn't matter if I'm in prison fifty years or two hours. If I turn rat, it's going to be a life sentence. So I think I'll just sit tight and see how things play out."

Claire moved closer to the cell. "You might want to worry about surviving *this* jail before you think about the future, Grumpy." She was standing directly in front of him, only the bars separating them.

"I think I'm going to do just fine in here."

His arm shot through the bars, his hand reaching for the gun on her hip. Claire's hand closed around his wrist before he could get her weapon. She pulled him hard against the bars, twisted his arm, and slapped his hand painfully against the metal. The sound he made was choked between a gasp of surprise and a shout of pain, and his face twisted in frustration.

"God, no wonder you're the first one I caught. You know who I am. You heard the stories. You know what I survived. Did you *really* think that *you* would be the one to end me?" She let go of his hand, shoving him away so he stumbled away from the bars. "I'm giving you a chance to come out of this better than any of those assholes. To save me a little trouble. If you're too stupid to see the opportunity, then I'm not going to waste any time on you."

"Stories. Heh." He shook his head. "You have stories. You think you're the first person who's tried to go after Den? You think this is where he started? The only reason he's here right now is because he's the best at what he does. I've seen cops, entire police departments, feds, try to take him down, and they all failed. Who are you? Some cop. You think you're going to scare me into giving up my guy? You can go fuck yourself."

Claire stared at him without blinking, then shook her head and walked away. "You want to burn along with your pals, fine. I kind of respect the loyalty of a rat fully embracing the ship as it sinks."

She left the cells. Randall was leaning against the wall but joined her again as she returned to the bullpen.

"I didn't catch all that, but it sounded intense. Are you sure you don't need help?"

"I'm going to say no right now," Claire said, "but I'll keep the offer in mind."

Randall went to reception while she went into her office and closed the door. She looked at the clock and did some mental math. The time zones didn't work in her favor, but she didn't want to wait until morning. She picked up the phone and dialed a number she knew by heart even though she'd sworn she would never use it. She sat down and closed her eyes, half-hoping there wouldn't be an answer.

There was a click, and she made a face so she wouldn't make a sound.

"This is Mallory."

"Faye. This is Claire."

She could almost hear Mallory waking up. She did hear the sound of blankets being pushed away, pajamas sliding across sheets. The silence stretched out long enough that Claire could imagine Mallory walking out of the bedroom before she said anything. Faye Mallory, Elaine's sister, the woman who was once going to be Claire's sister-in-law, the agent who made it her mission in life to chase Claire across the United States when she believed her to be responsible for Elaine's murder.

She was also the person who rallied the troops to speak up for Claire when she finally turned herself in. Mallory was the reason Claire was a free woman now. They mended their relationship as much as they could, but Claire knew Mallory still partially blamed her for Elaine's death. It never would have happened if Claire wasn't a cop, or if she hadn't blown her cover. Claire knew that because she felt the same way. They were civil on the extremely rare occasions they had to talk, but they'd never been and never would be friends.

It was going to make asking her for a favor incredibly awkward.

"Do you know what time it is?" Mallory asked.

"I do," Claire said, "and I apologize. But you know what it means, right? For me to be calling you at all, let alone in the middle of the night."

Mallory sighed heavily. "Yeah. Fill me in."

Claire recapped the past week as concisely as she could, then explained what she'd learned from Rucker's notebook. Mallory listened without interruption, but occasionally made noises of understanding. Claire could hear her sitting down, tapping on a keyboard, evidence she was taking notes. She wished she'd thought of Mallory before Grumpy mentioned the feds, but she wasn't going to waste time kicking herself over it.

"The name?" Mallory asked when Claire finished.

"Wyman, Dennis." She spelled it, then named the other men Rucker suspected as part of the group. "The man I have in custody is George Lile."

Mallory typed something. "Wyman has a big presence. Lots of suspicion, but nothing that stuck. He's been off the radar for a few years."

"Looks like he finally found a project that spoke to him."

"Let me send you some people. I can call in a few favors at the Seattle Field Office and you can have backup by morning."

Claire looked out the window. "That's not very likely. We're on the front edge of a blizzard here. I think the ferry is going to officially suspend service in the morning."

"Damn. I didn't know it got that cold up there."

"Climate change," Claire said.

"I guess." Mallory sighed. "So you're stuck. I know you, Lance, and I don't doubt~"

"Curran."

Mallory paused. "Excuse me?"

"Claire Curran." Silence. "People generally call me Claire now, but my last name is Curran. Jodie and I got married."

"Oh. Right, I knew that. Congratulations."

Claire regretted saying anything.

Mallory cleared her throat. "Well, whatever name you're going by, you're still the same person who joined a gang of bank robbers to protect the woman you loved. You're going to do something very noble and borderline stupid. Would it do any good to say to sit tight and wait for the thaw?"

"Probably not."

"Right. So instead I suppose I'll go with my second-best advice. Be careful. Wyman touches a lot of very hot stoves without getting burnt. He's probably clever, he's definitely dangerous."

Claire said, "I've fought dangerous and clever people before."

"Be that as it may," Mallory said. "Elaine would have wanted me to say it."

"Yeah," Claire said quietly. "Consider it noted."

"I'll put in the request on those names and email what we get as soon as we get it."

Claire said, "Thank you, Faye. How, um... how's Toni?"

"We don't have to make small talk," Mallory said. Another pause, and then with a slightly kinder tone. "She's fine. We're both doing well."

"Good. I'm glad to hear it."

"Jodie?"

"Good. She's good." She ran her finger along the edge of the desk, imagining Mallory doing something equally mundane to fill the silence. "Thank you for your help. I'll let you get back to sleep."

"Be careful. I mean it. You're used to doing this Lone Ranger thing because you didn't have options. You have a badge now. That comes with certain advantages. And restrictions."

"I'll keep that in mind. Good night, Faye."

"Goodnight, Claire."

She hung up and looked out her office window at Randall's back. Mallory was right. She had options, but she also had people who could be hurt or killed. In the old days, she took risks because she was only risking her own life. She leaned back in her chair and pushed her hands through her hair. That would be the real trial of this job, she realized. Randall, Harvey Moses, even Minnie and the other volunteers were at risk.

But that was the job. If she ever wanted to be a good sheriff, she'd have to find a way to accept the fact her people might suffer because of it.

***

There was a quiet knock on the office door just after daybreak. Claire was at the wall looking at a topographical map of the island, having marked the unnamed road where Wyman and his men were hiding out. The road was almost completely obscured by trees; she could only see it because she knew it was there. The houses were about a half-mile from the main road, surrounded by sparse woods, but anyone being held prisoner there would see it as an impenetrable forest.

Randall knocked again, then poked his head in without waiting to be invited inside. "Hey, boss. A civilian wants to have a word with you."

From behind him, out of sight, Jodie said, "Tell her the civilian brought coffee and doughnuts."

Claire frowned. "I don't want to give the impression we can be bribed."

"They're maple bacon," Jodie called.

"Let the bribery commence. Did you bring one for Randall?"

Randall said, "Oh, I already got my bribe back at the desk. How do you think she got this far?"

Claire shook her head. "I'll mark down your disloyalty in the ledger."

Randall stepped out of the way with a smile. Jodie came inside with a to-go bag from Coffee Table Books and greeted Claire with a kiss before she took a seat in front of the desk.

"How's traffic out there?" Claire asked.

"Actually not bad. No wind, the snow stopped falling, and it's supposed to get above freezing for a few hours around noon."

Claire pulled up a chair and sat down. Her knee bumped against Jodie's, but neither of them repositioned.

"That's good," Claire said as she accepted her doughnut. "Maybe it means the weather will break soon. We can get some people in here to help us deal with Wyman."

Jodie shook her head and swallowed her bite before she spoke. "Not likely. The internet said ferry service is suspended for at least two days because of icing. And that's if things don't get worse, which they might, because this is just a little breather before the real storm. Plummeting temperatures, more freezing rain and snow. It's going to be a hell of a weekend."

"Damn," Claire said. "At least that means Wyman and his guys are frozen out, too."

"Have you made any progress on that?"

Claire said, "I called Faye and asked for some FBI assistance. I should have everything I need to know on these guys in a few hours." She gestured at the map. "I was trying to see what shoreline was closest to their camp and would also be safe enough for multiple landings."

Jodie said, "Oh. Here I was hoping you'd taken advantage of the standby room for at least a couple of hours."

"I tried sleeping, Jodie, but I just lie there and think about what I could be doing for the case~"

"You want to know what you can do for the case?" Jodie snapped. "You can rest your body. You can let your brain recharge. You lie awake thinking of what you can do, and I lie awake thinking about what will happen if you slip. If you're not at a hundred percent at the wrong moment, you could be too slow, you could die, because your brain was foggy or you weren't paying complete attention. I want you to *sleep*, Claire, I want you to be ready for whatever happens, and why is that such a fucking big thing to ask?"

She deflated when she finished speaking, her elbow on the desk, hand on her forehead. Claire stared at her, stunned and silent, fully chastised. She thought about George grabbing for her gun, and if she'd been half a second slower in springing her trap. She'd been so confident that she would be faster than he was that she'd stepped right into a very dangerous position.

"You brought me coffee..."

"I brought you decaf," Jodie said weakly.

Claire smiled. "Clever lady."

"You don't have to sleep for eight hours." She swiped at her eyes in case any tears had slipped free. "Just lie down, in a real bed, with the lights out. Stay there for a little while. That's all I ask."

"Okay. I can rest in the standby room and let Randall cover things for a bit."

"Thank you."

Claire stood up and bent down to kiss some brown sugar from Jodie's top lip. "Thank *you*. You're obviously right. I love you. And I've been pushing myself too hard this week. The burn-out was going to happen sooner or later, and I can't risk it happening when I'm going against someone like Wyman."

"You're welcome," Jodie said. "And I love you."

"I suppose you'll be standing guard outside the room to make sure I don't sneak out."

Jodie said, "As much as I would love that, I can't. I have to go to work. Everyone is taking advantage of today to prepare for being snowed in. That means getting their cars serviced, which means the garage is already running behind and it's not even officially open yet. But luckily *I'm* fully rested and ready for a full day of hard work."

"Show off." Claire finished her coffee and grimaced. "I must be off. How did I not realize that was decaf? Wow."

Jodie stood up and put her hands flat on Claire's shoulders. "I'm going so I can get the garage ready. And the earlier I leave, the more sleep you get."

"You can tell Randall to babysit me. Send you reports every hour."

"I would love that. I'll tell him on my way out." She kissed Claire's lips. "I love you."

"I love you," Claire said. "Now go... I want to take a nap."

Jodie smiled. "Yes, ma'am."

Claire watched her go and finished her doughnut. When she left her office, she went to where Randall was sitting and put a hand on his shoulder.

"Did Jodie tell you your mission?"

"She did indeed. I'm going to follow orders, because she brings the good doughnuts. Also I'm more scared of her than I am of you."

She patted his shoulder. "Smart. Very smart. I want you to call some people, see if any of our lovely volunteers are willing to camp out here when things get rough again. We'll provide them with food and anything else they might need, but I want people here to watch our guest."

"You got it. I already got a verbal promise from Harvey Moses that he'll take over for me when I head home, so he'll be my first call."

"He's a good man."

"Mm-hmm," Randall said. "Uh, not to be a buzzkill, boss, but I want to be able to give Mrs. Curran a good report..."

"Yeah, yeah, yeah, I'm going."

She walked away, forcing herself not to look back when the phone rang. The standby room was more accurately a closet with an army surplus cot, a wool blanket, and two pillows. Its main appeal was a lack of windows and distance from the bullpen so the phones were less of a distraction. She took off her belt and placed it on a shelf, untucked and unbuttoned her uniform shirt and hung it in the small portable wardrobe. She paused and ran her fingers over the cold metal star on the shirt's breast pocket.

Jodie called the badge "your armor," and the gun was "your sword." Once it had felt unusual to put them on, to call herself a police officer again after so long spent on the other side of the law. Now she felt exposed without them.

Claire sat on the cot, toed off her shoes, and laid down. She heard Randall's voice as a comforting rumble echoing down the hall. He sounded calm and in control. She put one hand behind her head, the other on her stomach, and crossed her feet at the ankle. She didn't think she would actually sleep, didn't think she actually needed to. Just lying down and taking a breather was restorative enough. It would do the trick and she could get back to work.

Maybe it wouldn't hurt if she closed her eyes...

Just for a second.

CHAPTER SEVEN

IF JODIE hadn't heard the weather report warning of a second storm front, she would have easily believed the worst was over. Plows had been out before dawn to clear the streets. Kids and even some adults were playing in the resulting mountain ranges that stood on each sidewalk. The businesses which had seemed so abandoned the past few days were now thriving, and she regretted there wasn't time to run in the general store to get some supplies.

When she got to the garage, there were already cars parked in front of all three bays. The doors were up and she saw Travis wave in the next customer as she pulled around to the employee parking lot. She hadn't been looking to run a garage when they moved to the island. She would've been happy to just be one of the greasers down in the maintenance floor, and that was what she was hired for. But then the guy who hired her started getting lazy. He saw how good she was at the job and started giving her more and more of his responsibilities. Eventually she was doing ninety percent of his job without any of the benefits.

Fortunately, the other employees saw what was happening and took action. She thought "coup" was too strong a word, but they joined together and told the owner that if he didn't resign so Jodie could have the job she deserved, they would all walk out and never return. He wisely chose to leave, and Jodie took over with one stipulation: she would be co-manager, and whoever shared the title took over the paperwork part of the job so she could keep her hands in the engines.

Kevin, the man who had agreed to share the manager title, walked out to meet her, turning to walk beside her as she came into the garage. "How's the missus?" he asked.

"Finally listening to reason," she said. "How are things here?"

"Barely-managed chaos. Everyone wants their shit checked out 'fore the big storm hits. They want to make sure the engines don't freeze to death sitting in the garages."

Jodie said, "Always nice to keep up with maintenance checks. Where do you need me the most?"

"Pinch-hitting," he said. "We've got a pretty good rhythm going, but keep your eye out for anyone who might be falling behind, lend a hand where it's needed."

"You got it, chief," she said.

Over the next hour, she helped with two engine checks and changed the oil on Cheryl Paxton's car. She had just finished putting a set of snow tires on Sara Tamirova's Jeep when she spotted a guy loitering outside on the grass, just next to the bay doors. He was wearing a heavy black jacket, but his bald head was exposed to the cold. He gave a nervous smile and lifted one hand when he realized she'd seen him. She slipped the lug wrench into the pocket of her overalls and made her way over to him.

"Hi. Can I help you?"

He jerked a thumb over his shoulder. "My car literally just crapped out on me. I know you've got a ton of customers here, and I'm not trying to jump the line, but it's honestly not moving an inch. If you could come take a look and at least give me an idea what's going on... My family is in the car and it's freezing, and—"

Jodie was already nodding. "Sure, it's no problem. I can take a look." She indicated for him to lead the way, and he walked beside her.

"Really?" He looked utterly relieved. "Thank you so much."

"No problem."

He pointed to the street that ran alongside the garage. She saw a car parked at the curb, the only vehicle on this particular street, but it was idling. It was also occupied by at least three adult men, two of which were in the backseat on the driver's side. The third man was at the wheel, his hand wrapped around the twelve o'clock position.

Jodie slowed and backed up a step. "Oh, actually, I should tell my boss I'm stepping out for a second."

The man grabbed her bicep and squeezed hard. All kindness was gone from his voice as he yanked her forward again.

"I think they'll be fine," he grunted.

There were certain benefits to being married to a cop. The pertinent one, in this moment, was that she knew having him grab her arm meant that anything she did now could reasonably be claimed as self-defense. She went limp and let herself slump to one side, which forced him to compensate by putting all his weight on one leg. He'd been walking on her left so he could grab her with his dominant hand. The downside was that it left her dominant hand free. She pulled the curved metal lug wrench from her pocket.

Another perk of marrying a cop: she knew to make contact on the upswing, putting all the energy into the blow. The circular end of the wrench came up quick and cracked off his chin loud enough to echo. She tensed her legs again, planted one foot on the snowy ground, and stomped the other down on the ankle he'd just shifted his weight to. It bent in a way that was very, very wrong, and he shrieked.

He was still holding onto her arm as he fell, so she smacked his fingers with the wrench. The way the middle one bent, she was positive it was broken, but she didn't care much about that.

"*Travis!*"

He was already running toward her, alerted by the goon's scream. She pointed at the man with her wrench. "Watch this asshole!" Then she turned and ran full-speed toward the car.

The driver pulled away fast enough to squeal the tires. Jodie changed her angle, pumping her arms, the metal of the wrench glinting each time it came up into her line of sight. She leapt over a snow dune and skidded a little when she hit the other side, but she stayed on her feet. The car was too far ahead for her to catch it, but she saw enough of the license plate before they screeched around a corner to hopefully make a difference.

She stopped chasing, knowing it would be a wasted effort, and reluctantly turned to go back. Travis had gotten the would-be kidnapper into a seated position, but he didn't seem to be attempting any sort of comfort. A group of customers and mechanics had gathered at the bay doors and seemed to be trying to make sense of what had just happened. Travis looked up when he heard Jodie approaching and smiled widely.

"Gah-damn, boss, you fucked this dude up!"

"Remember that the next time you're late, Travis." The adrenaline was starting to wear off, so she put the wrench back in her pocket so her shaking hands would be less noticeable. To the gawkers, she shouted, "Has anyone called the police?"

Kevin called back, "We thought we'd leave that up to you. Seeing as you have the personal connection and all."

Travis held out his phone to her, and she took it. "Yeah... nice to have connections with the local law enforcement."

***

"I just don't understand why Claire isn't here," Randall said.

They were seated on the couch in the cramped office she shared with Kevin. Harvey Moses had climbed into the ambulance with the attempted kidnapper. She was holding a cup of coffee with both hands, watching the buzz of activity outside through the open door. The excitement of the attempted abduction was already forgotten by everyone else, and she really just wanted to get back to work.

"I literally *just* got her to bed, and I'm not about to be the one who wakes her up. She was still asleep when you left?" He nodded. "Okay. You're good enough to handle this."

He put a hand over his heart. "Your confidence in me is so overwhelming, I might cry." He removed his hand, put it on her shoulder. "Seriously, though. You're sure you're okay?"

"Yes. All he did was grab my arm. He's the one who had to be taken away in an ambulance. Did I really break his ankle?"

"Uh, the word the medic actually used was 'shatter,' so yeah, I'd say you broke it. I didn't like the way that finger was swelling, either. You kicked some solid ass today, Mrs. Boss, well done."

Jodie grunted. "I just wish I'd been able to get more of the license plate."

Randall looked down at his notepad. "Four digits with a make and model isn't nothing. We'll see what we can get on it."

"You mean *you'll* see."

He stared at her. "You have to tell Claire about this."

"I'm... I don't..."

He lowered his voice. "Whatever is going on here, whatever big case Rucker was working on and whatever has Claire staying up for three days straight, those guys are definitely connected to it somehow. Even if they weren't, and even if you weren't Claire's wife, there's no way I could keep something like this from the sheriff."

"I know." She sighed and rubbed her face. "She's going to freak out."

Randall shook his head. "She's going to worry. That's not necessarily a bad thing to get from a partner."

"Yeah. Yeah, I know. Don't let her do anything insane, Randall. If she finds out they came after me, she might take the gloves off."

"I'll watch out for her. You have my word."

"Thank you." She stood up and went to the desk. "What's going to happen with the guy who went to the hospital?"

Randall said, "He had ID on him. Teddy Packard. Harvey Moses is going to stay with him while he's at the hospital. I don't know what we'll do after that. I don't really like the idea of putting him in the same cell as his buddy, but there's nowhere else to put him. If we start arresting more people, we're going to have to deputize more people just to stand guard."

"Claire will figure something out," Jodie said.

"I hope." Randall stood and patted the notebook against his hip. "I'll take this back, see what I find. But Jodie..."

She nodded. "I know. You have to. But try to break it to her easy, all right?"

"Kind of like, 'hope you had a nice nap, boss, let's see, there was a fender bender, a slip and fall outside the library, your wife almost got abducted, and Dan Porter ran a stop sign. Nice quiet morning.'"

"Sounds right to me."

He chuckled and waved as he left the office. Jodie stood up and closed the door behind him. She rested her head against the wood, took a breath, and suffered a sudden and violent full-body shudder. She could still feel Packard's grip on her arm. She rubbed the spot through her shirt and walked back toward the desk.

She fell in love with Claire Lance before she knew her real name. They met in a grungy little garage in Shepherd, Washington. At first Claire, then using the name Carmen Landry, was just another pair of hands to take some of the workload. Then she was a friend. When she became more, Claire revealed the truth. She was a fugitive, on the run for murder, a dangerous person to be around, let alone fall in love with. By that point, Jodie didn't care. A part of her knew that even if Claire had been guilty of the crimes she was accused of committing, she still would have stuck by her side.

Claire put her freedom and her life on the line to protect Jodie. She took Jodie's place in a bank robbery that went horribly wrong, and it could have ended with Claire being sent to prison for good. And still Jodie stayed. She stayed through Claire's faked death, the long periods of silence when Claire was hiding out somewhere and couldn't safely get in touch. She gave up the idea of being settled and spent weekends on Squire's Isle, she moved to Alaska, and finally decided to join Claire on the run.

Jodie threw out ideas like safety and stability for the danger of always being on the move. If the wrong person recognized Claire, it would all be over. And Jodie probably would have gone down as well for aiding and abetting.

"I can't promise you anything," Claire said.

They were on the road. It was a little past one in the morning, but neither of them were tired. All they could see was a stretch of highway caught in their headlights. They were passing through a sleeping town, but it could literally have been any of a thousand American towns. Storage units, gas stations, big department stores, and the all-night shine of familiar fast foot logos.

"Literally, nothing," Claire emphasized. "I can't promise we'll have enough money for gas tomorrow. Or that we'll have both lunch and dinner tomorrow. I can't promise that we won't be doing this six months from now. Or... a year from now. This may be forever, Calico."

"I know," Jodie said.

Claire sounded exasperated. "Do you? Because really, the only way it stops is with one or both of us in prison. That's not appealing, of course, but can you take roads like this for the rest of your life?"

Jodie sat up straighter. "Can you promise you'll wait for me before you leave the next gas station?"

"What? Yeah, of course."

"Can you promise that if we can only afford one shitty fast food meal, you'll cut the burger in half and share the fries with me?"

"Jodie..."

"Promise, Ms. Lance."

Claire flexed her fingers on the steering wheel. "I promise. Of course I do."

Jodie looked out the car window. "This isn't how I pictured my life. I didn't imagine hotels, Goodwill clothes stuffed in the backseat, driving nine days out of ten." She turned and looked at Claire, whose profile was lit by the console and passing streetlights. "But I didn't imagine you, either. I didn't imagine anything close to you. So it's worth it, Claire. It's worth it."

She smiled at the memory. Uncertainty and danger were part of life with Claire Lance Curran. A few scary nights, some worry and stress, the need to be alert and aware of her surroundings sometimes. It was a small price to pay for the honor of waking up next to her every morning.

The pain in her arm had faded, and she patted her bicep as she pushed away from the desk. She would finish as much work as she could before Claire woke up and learned what had happened. She had a feeling that storm would be a lot more dangerous than anything Mother Nature had in store for them over the weekend.

***

The light coming in through the front windows had changed significantly when Claire emerged from the standby room. Minnie had arrived while she was asleep, and Randall had relocated to his usual desk. She saw two volunteers, Chip Ewing and Fred Hill, were also present. They were both wearing the dark brown polo shirts with SQUIRE'S ISLE POLICE stitched on the breast in gold thread. Both men were single and seemed likely candidates for camping out if necessary. They both nodded to her when she came into the bullpen.

"You guys here for the long haul?"

"As long as you need us, Cl- Sheriff."

She resisted the urge to sigh. "If you guys are more comfortable calling me Claire, I'm all for it. I know it's weird for you to say, and it's weird for me to hear." She turned to Randall, who had jumped up to stand next to her like an excited child. "What's going on with you?"

He gestured toward her office. Chip and Fred looked down, suddenly interested in nonexistent paperwork. Claire led the way, and Randall closed the office door behind them. He turned to face her.

"Did you ever see Memento?"

"I don't know what that is."

"It's this movie that tells the story backward. Like, it starts at the end, and each scene is actually what happened before what you just saw."

Claire raised her eyebrows. "That sounds stupid."

"No, it was great. It's, um, not relevant. I'm going to tell you what happened today, but I'm going to start with the end, then work my way backward. Okay?"

She crossed her arms over her chest. "Okay."

"We have another one of Wyman's guys in custody."

"That's fantastic. Is he here now? Who's watching him?"

Randall said, "Harvey Moses is watching him. The reason he's not in one of our cells is because he's in the hospital."

"What's he doing in the hospital?"

"Shattered ankle and broken jaw."

Claire furrowed her brow. "Who the hell did that?"

"Jodie."

"*Jodie?*" She advanced on him. "What the hell was... How'd..."

Randall held his hands up. "Okay. Okay. It's okay, Jodie is fine. The guy, Teddy Packard, tried to grab Jodie at the garage. She stomped on his ankle and used a lug wrench to break his face." He couldn't resist a little smile. "All the witnesses said it was pretty badass. She got a partial license plate, but it's just another rental car registered to Wyman. She said there were three guys in the car, but she didn't get a good look at any of them."

Claire pointed at the pictures from Rucker's file. "I imagine they looked just like that." The rage was still boiling at the back of her mind, but she held it back. "Which one is Packard?"

"Oh." Randall picked up a Sharpie and identified the proper photo. "So that's good news. We have names for three out of the six."

"Names doesn't do us much good, and it doesn't help the women they're holding right now. Where is Jodie?"

"She stayed at work." Sensing her reaction, he quickly added, "It was her decision. Tell me I would've had a shot of talking her out of it."

Claire sighed. "Right." She paced toward the window. "We need to tell Mayor Hood-Colby about this while we have the chance. We don't need any kind of search warrant because there's no way Wyman is the legal owner of those houses, but I want an official okay before we start stomping all over the land. Without a judge, the mayor is the most authority we can hope for. You said Jodie was okay?"

"She's absolutely fine, Claire. You have my word."

"All right. Okay. I'll go talk to the mayor right now."

"Uh, boss? In a way, we're pretty lucky that Packard got hurt. If he weren't in the hospital, we'd have to stick him in one of the cells right alongside George. If we start arresting more of these guys, we're going to have an overcrowding issue."

It was a concern she'd had in the back of her mind, but not one she'd come up with a solution for. "We'll worry about that when we catch more of them," she said. "Thanks, Randall."

"You got it. Boss?" Claire turned to look at him. "You should watch *Memento*. It really is a good movie."

She rolled her eyes and couldn't stop herself from chuckling.

Claire put on her coat and the Stetson. As she left the building, she took out her cell phone and dialed Jodie's number. It buzzed once.

"I had a feeling you might call."

"Are you *positive* you're~"

"I'm okay, Claire. Honest." The sound of engine work was suddenly muted, and Claire assumed she had stepped into the office. "I'm a little buzzed on adrenaline, but once that wears off..."

Claire paused at the doors of City Hall. "Do you need anything?"

"No, I'm good. Can I put a hug on layaway, though?"

"It'll be waiting the next time I see you."

Jodie chuckled. "That's what I need. I should go. I love you."

"I love you, too."

She hung up, took a breath to settle herself, then went inside. The lobby was almost stifling after the cold air of outside. The heat was on full blast, and the combined body heat of people paying fines and water bills made it feel like a sauna. The people talked loudly to be heard over other people talking loudly as they all tried to make sure everything was settled just in case they were snowed in. She headed upstairs and found the mayor's secretary was gone but the office door was open. She knocked as she went inside, taking off her hat.

"Mayor?"

Patricia was standing at the desk. She looked up to see who it was, then went back to gathering the papers on her blotter.

"Sheriff Curran. Do you mind walking and talking? I'm embarrassingly late for a meeting."

"Can you be very late for it?"

Patricia paused. "That depends. What's going on?"

"I think someone is using the island for human trafficking. The girls arrive on the western shore, our guy grabs them up, and he takes them to the mainland one by one to avoid suspicion."

"Shit." Patricia took off her glasses and put the papers back down. She picked up her phone, punched an extension, and tapped her finger against the receiver as it rang. "Toby? Hi. I won't be there. You can take over as my proxy. Yes. Thank you." She hung up and sat down, gesturing for Claire to do the same. "Okay, Sheriff. Tell me what you know."

Claire took a seat and put the Stetson on the arm of the chair. Patricia listened silently as she carefully explained everything she'd learned since Rucker's death.

"I can't prove any of this," she admitted when she got to the end, "but the pieces fit. And even if I'm wrong about who those girls are in the photos, Wyman can't be up to anything good in those abandoned houses."

Patricia said, "I absolutely agree. And you're positive your wife is okay?"

Claire tensed. "I haven't seen her, but Randall said she's fine. He wouldn't sugarcoat it if she wasn't. But I plan to go talk with her after I leave here."

"And how are you doing? I don't want to dredge up bad memories, but I... I know what happened to Elaine. It can't be easy to have another bad person trying to use the woman you love against you."

"I appreciate the concern, but I... I don't..." She looked at the frost-covered window until she regained her composure. "I can't afford to think like that right now, Patricia."

Patricia nodded. "I only brought it up because we have a spare room. Jill and I, at the mayor's residence. The property has a wall. And a gate. If you and Jodie want to camp out until this is all taken care of, we're great hosts."

Claire lowered her head to look at her shoes, completely stumped about why she was being so emotional. Finally she just nodded.

"We're happy to do it. I don't want to give these assholes the chance to try again." She took out her cell phone. "I'll call Jill and ask her to set up the room when she has a chance."

"Thank you."

"These guys tried to abduct a woman in broad daylight. And if your suspicions are right, they also killed Cal when he started making moves against them. I'm not losing anyone else, and I don't want you pulling your punches." She hit a button on her phone and put it to her ear. "I've heard the song they wrote about you, Claire, and I feel lucky to have you looking out for us here."

Claire said, "For the record, I hate that song."

"Yeah, we all hate it when people write songs about how awesome we are." She winked and then reacted to her call being answered. "Jill... hey. Are you at home...?"

They arranged for the room to be ready for Jodie to move in that night, and Claire promised she would join her. It wasn't hiding, she told herself. It was being smart, savvy, retreating behind the castle walls in order to regroup and come up with a strategy. She thanked Patricia again and stood to leave.

"One more thing, Sheriff," Patricia said.

Claire turned around at the door.

Patricia smiled. "I love the hat."

Claire looked at the Stetson, then self-consciously put it on. "Jodie's idea. I'm sure it'll grow on me." She touched the brim. "Thank you again, Patricia."

"This is our home. We've got to look out for each other. You go get 'em, Lance."

Claire usually corrected people when they called her that. It was an old name, a name that belonged to a folk hero, a celebrity, someone who didn't exist anymore.

But just this once, she thought she'd let it slide.

CHAPTER EIGHT

CLAIRE HAD been very impressed by the island's hospital when she first arrived. She'd expected a glorified clinic, perfectly serviceable but unable to handle bigger emergencies. In reality, she found a three-story care center that rivaled some of the hospitals she'd seen in much larger cities. "We have to do as much as we can," one of the doctors once told her, "because we're too far away to call for back-up. If we try sending a patient to Seattle for emergency care, odds are good they won't survive the trip. We're their only hope."

As she entered the gleaming blue cube of the lobby, she spotted Dr. Rachel Crawford at the nurse's station. Rachel was a petite Asian woman who had the ability to make everyone feel like she was taller than they were. She walked with her shoulders back and chin high and moved with such authority that most people couldn't help but see her as their superior. She was also the wife of Alexandra Crawford, the fire chief.

She saw Claire and excused herself from the conversation she was having, crossing the lobby. She changed direction so they were walking shoulder to shoulder.

"I assume you're here to see the prisoner."

"If that's okay with you."

"Fine with me," Rachel said, "but I don't think you're going to get much out of him."

Claire said, "Stubborn?"

"Probably. But your wife *shattered* his jaw. It's going to be a long time before he speaks again, and even then he might end up with a speech impediment."

"I'll scold Jodie for her ruthlessness."

Rachel said, "You'd better." Her lips curled into a smile.

They were in an empty stretch of hallway, so Claire put up a hand to stop Rachel. "How's Alex doing? She and Rucker worked together for a long time. Finding him must not have been easy."

"Yeah, it wasn't." Rachel's mood sobered. "She's doing well. Sleepless nights, you know, loss of appetite. The sort of thing you'd expect from working a colleague's death. But she knew the two of you were closer, so it would have been worse for you. She was more than willing to take the relatively softer blow to protect you from a knock-out."

Claire nodded. "Tell her I appreciate it."

"Tell her yourself. Over dinner, sometime when the weather is better."

"Deal."

They continued around the corner and Rachel pointed at a closed door. "Your man is in there. He's in a pretty foul mood. Go make it worse."

"I'll do my best. Thanks, Rachel."

"Mm-hmm." She started back the way they'd come. "Give my love to your love. And tell her the garage should have security cameras outside."

"They tried to abduct her in broad daylight. I don't think they would have been scared away by a few cameras."

"Screw that. I just wish I could see the footage." She mimed a Babe Ruth swing, made a 'that must have hurt face,' and waved her fingers as she rounded the corner.

Claire went into the room. Harvey Moses had pulled a chair over to sit at the foot of the bed, facing the prisoner. Packard looked like he'd been dropped into the bed from a great height and didn't bother to rearrange himself. Harvey Moses glanced at Claire as she came in, nodded, and then looked back at Packard. He was glaring at her, one corner of his lip pulled up in what probably would have been a sneer if his face wasn't so swollen and bruised.

"Boss."

"Hey, Harv," she said. "Are you boys getting along?"

"Oh yeah. He's not much of a conversationalist, but we're enjoying each other's company a lot."

She said, "Great to hear it. Why don't you stretch your legs?"

Harvey Moses looked at Packard. "No, I'm... I'm pretty good right here."

She broke the staring contest. "I mean it, Harvey Moses. Go for a walk. Get a snack."

"The nurses have been bringing me whatever I need. I'm good."

"Then go pee," she said sharply.

He looked at Packard. He stood up and moved closer to Claire. "Boss, you know how much I respect you and all that. But I really don't think I should leave you alone with him."

"He's cuffed to the bed."

"Yeah. He's not the one I'm worried about. I think if you were thinking clearly, you'd want me in here. Just in case."

Claire met his eye. "I understand. But I still want you to go."

Harvey Moses sighed. He looked at Packard, then shrugged. "I'll take a stroll. But I'll be back."

"Thanks," she said.

He left the door open behind him, a not-so-subtle signal, but Claire pushed it shut. She watched through the narrow window next to the door to make sure he actually went down the hall. Once he was gone, she turned and looked at Packard.

"My wife," she said.

Packard glared at her.

She walked forward. "Wyman went after my wife. He sent *you* to do it. I don't care if it wasn't your idea. It's your face she's going to see when she thinks about it. And I want you to think about her every time you look at the new shape of your face. Because this...?" She waved a finger toward his jaw. "That's going to do some permanent damage to your looks. She'll take comfort in that. That's what she's going to hold onto when you try creeping into her nightmares. She'll see your fucked-up face. She'll hear the sound your ankle made when it snapped. And she'll go back to sleep and dream of driving fast with the wind in her hair.

"But I don't have that, Teddy. Your face is in my head, too, but I didn't see you get hit or hear your bone break, so I can't use that to make you go away." She leaned in closer, almost close enough for him to lunge at her. She lowered her voice to almost a whisper. "So that's what I'm going to think about, Ted. How to get rid of the man who went after my wife."

He cleared his throat. He kept his eyes locked on hers, but there was a tightening at the corners that told her he was scared.

She straightened and put some distance between them. "So we have you. George Lile. And Dennis Wyman. All I need are three more names. Jodie left your hands alone, so you can write or type whatever you want. Three names. If you give them to me, that might make me like you a little bit. We'll never be friends. But it'll at least get you off my mind."

She took a pen and pad from her pocket. She ripped off a page, put it on his bedside tray, and pushed it over his torso. He stared at the paper for a second, then picked up the pen and started writing. Claire waited until he was done and had slapped down the pen before she moved closer. She craned her neck and looked at what he'd written.

"Clark Kent, Luke Skywalker, and Mickey Mouse. You could be telling the truth. Stranger things have happened, I guess. I once knew a guy in Chicago named Mason Perry. You know, like Perry Mason, but~ never mind, probably before your time."

She took back her pen and paper.

"George didn't want to play along, either. He was a real asshole about it, too. But I did eventually learn his name. I'm going to learn the names of your friends, too. And you're not going to get credit for helping out. That's a shame. Because you are starting at such a huge deficit, you should be taking all the bonuses you're offered."

Teddy muttered something, but his teeth never moved apart.

"I'm going to assume that was derogatory," Claire said.

Harvey Moses came back. He looked at the bed, clearly relieved to see Packard was still in one piece and hadn't suffered any further damage.

"Hey, Harvey Moses," Claire said.

"Hey." He handed her a bag of Raisinets. "You two have a nice chat?"

"Thank you," she said as she opened the candy. "Yeah, we got to know each other pretty well, didn't we, Teddy?" To Harvey Moses, she said, "Are you okay to stay here with him until we get you some relief?"

"Oh, yeah. He can help me with the crossword."

She nodded and patted his shoulder. "Call the barn if you need us to bring you anything."

"You got it."

She gave Packard one last look before she left.

He was the one who looked away.

***

Claire was in the bedroom packing a bag when Jodie got home. It took every bit of willpower she had to stay away from the garage, to physically confirm Jodie was okay, but she knew that if she did that she'd never be able to leave.

So she stayed at the station and went through the records Mallory had sent her. Wyman was clean ("Suspiciously clean," Mallory said in the email, "for someone who hangs out with criminals."), but Lile had a beefy rap sheet. Grand theft auto, destruction of property, domestic abuse charges, public indecency, public drunkenness, all sorts of assholery. She requested Theodore Packard's record and found plenty of information without bringing the FBI into it. Teddy was well known by the Seattle police for various instances of petty larceny. Apparently, he thought he was ready to graduate up to abductions.

Claire put all thoughts of them out of her mind as soon as she heard the front door close. "I'm in here," she called. She was still mostly in uniform, though she'd taken off the blouse and was wearing a plain white undershirt. She'd also untied her hair so it hung loose on her shoulders.

Jodie cautiously came into the bedroom, pausing at the threshold. "Hey..."

"Hey." Claire frowned. "What's wrong?"

"Are you mad?"

"Mad? About…"

"I fucked up your case. Randall told me he can't talk. If I hadn't–"

Claire laughed and crossed the room to take Jodie into her arms. "You could have knocked his damn head off and I wouldn't give a damn. You were so amazing today." She stepped back and looked her over. "Are you sure you're okay? Did your arm bruise?"

"No, it's fine." She rubbed the spot through her sleeve. "I was just nervous because you never came by to check on me."

"You said… I thought…"

Jodie shook her head. "I know. I don't know why, and I know that you probably assumed I wanted you to stay away. I would have sent you away if you *had* shown up. But the more time passed without seeing you, I thought, well, maybe…"

Claire kissed Jodie between the eyebrows. "I will never be mad at you for defending yourself. You're my hero."

"Where's the asshole now?"

Claire squeezed Jodie's uninjured shoulder and pulled away to go back to the suitcase. "Hospital. He's refusing to cooperate even in writing, so I don't think it matters that you broke his jaw."

"I guess that makes me feel a little less guilty." She looked at the suitcase. "Sorry, where are you going?"

"We're going to the mayor's residence."

"With a suitcase?"

Claire looked at her. "Yeah. Patricia offered. Given everything that's happened, I thought it would be better to err on the side of caution. They have a wall and a gate. It's not likely anyone will get close enough to try anything."

Jodie crossed her arms over her chest. "Claire, I'm not leaving my home."

"Yes, you are. We are. Just until this whole thing with Wyman is settled."

"This is our home." She raised her voice slightly. "You're going to let these guys run us out of our home?"

Claire went back to her. "These guys have the kind of records you don't mess around with. And that's just the two we've been able to catch. Who knows what the others are capable of? I'm not taking the chance."

"I won't let these guys run me from my home."

Claire snapped, "And *I* won't walk in to find someone else I love…" She caught herself, the shouted words dying in a choked sob. She twisted away from Jodie and put a hand over her face. She was shaking everywhere. All she could see was a bloody bed and Elaine Mallory's wide-open eyes. Nausea threatened to overtake her but she fought it down, compromising with a ragged sob.

She didn't remember dropping to her knees, but she felt Jodie's arms going around her, pulling her close.

"I'm sorry," Jodie whispered. "I wasn't thinking about her."

Claire found one of Jodie's hands with hers and squeezed. "I can't lose you, Jodie. I just barely survived losing Elaine. If I lost you..."

"You won't." Jodie squeezed Claire tighter and kissed her hair. "I'll go. I'll go."

"Thank you."

They sat on the floor together until Claire felt like herself again. Jodie whispered, "Come here," and helped her up to the foot of the bed. They sat next to each other and Jodie moved her lips to Claire's neck. Claire closed her eyes and hummed softly, appreciating the tender kisses until she noticed Jodie was working the button on her pants.

"Jodie...?"

"I was almost abducted today. I've been buzzed ever since it happened." She moved her lips to kiss Claire's jaw. "I just need to be reminded I survived. And I'm not going to have sex with the mayor down the hall, so tonight is our only chance. I can do it myself in the shower if you're not~"

"No." Claire took Jodie's hand, guiding it into her pants. She lifted her hips and turned her head. Their lips met and Jodie repositioned her wrist to get a better angle. Claire started to lean back, easing Jodie's body so she would end up on laying on top of her.

Something shattered outside.

Jodie jerked her hand back as Claire fastened her pants, both jumping up and moving toward the door.

"Jodie..."

"Don't tell me to hide."

"No. I was going to tell you to stay by me in case that was a distraction."

Claire retrieved her gun from the belt she'd discarded earlier and led the way out of the bedroom. Tires screeched on the road, but that didn't mean the threat was gone. She paused at the doorway to the living room and watched Jodie run into the kitchen. She retrieved one of the stainless steel knives from the wooden block next to the stove. Claire remembered unwrapping those knives on Christmas morning, a gift honoring her then-newfound love of cooking. The word CURRAN was written in gold script on the handles.

She pushed those thoughts away to focus on the current threat. Jodie came back to her, nodding that she was ready for whatever might happen. Claire opened the front door, swept the porch to confirm it was clear, and stepped out onto the snowy lawn.

Her squad car was on fire.

The driver's side window was broken, and bright orange flames curled up over the roof. More fire bloomed across the front and back seats. Steam rose from the frost that had accumulated on the car's body since she got home, and the snow around it was quickly evaporating into puddles of shimmering water. It would have been beautiful under other circumstances, but Claire only searched the area for signs of the arsonist.

"Stay close to the wall," she told Jodie as she ran across the lawn. Her socks were immediately soaked through and her toes were numb as she stood on the edge of the road and looked in both directions. There were no tracks since the road had been plowed earlier in the day.

"Claire?"

"Yeah," she said, turning back toward the house.

Jodie was staring at the burning car. "I think I'm ready to move into the mayor's residence."

"Yeah."

Claire checked the lawn again to make sure no one was lurking in the shadows. They'd go inside, she would double-check every door and window while Jodie called the fire department, and then they would get the hell out of the house.

***

The town's volunteer firefighters managed to extinguish the fire without much trouble, but the squad car was left as a smoldering ruin in the aftermath. Plumes of grey smoke swirled up into the air. Claire noticed the low clouds had returned, and assumed snow would start falling by morning. She and Jodie were on the porch of their house as Alex Crawford examined the scene. The chief was off-duty but had arrived in her personal vehicle when she heard what was going on.

Claire had used the time before their arrival to take photos of the driveway and lawn. Most of the snow around the car had melted, but she managed to get shots of a few scattered footprints that didn't belong to her or Jodie.

When the fire was out and Alex had a chance to examine the remains, she walked over to join them on the porch.

"Very preliminary, nothing written down, but I would say this is arson."

"I won't quote you on that, Chief," Claire said.

Alex smiled wryly and gestured at the driver's side window. "They broke the glass with a stone, which is lying on the passenger seat, then tossed in a bottle that shattered against the steering wheel. Then they lit a match and..." She made an explosion with her hands. "Are you two okay?"

"We're fine. We have a place to stay tonight. Deputy Ewing is going to watch the house to make sure they don't come back."

"Do you need a ride to where you're staying?"

Claire nodded. "That would be appreciated. Thank you."

She put the bags in the back of Alex's truck and called to make sure the Hood-Colbys were ready for their arrival. Then she and Jodie squeezed into the truck next to Alex and headed out. Jodie twisted to look over her shoulder at their house, and Claire squeezed her hand as soon as it was out of sight.

The mayor's wife, Jill, was waiting in the door when Alex pulled through the gate. "Swanky sort of safe house," she said under her breath.

"Maybe you'll get lucky and someone will try to kill you soon."

"Been there, done that," Alex said. "I like a quiet, boring life."

Jill came out onto the porch, and Claire saw that a little girl had been peeking around the corner of the doorway behind her. Alex apologized for dumping them and running, but she wanted to get back to finish securing the scene at their house.

"Claire, Jodie." She smiled and greeted Jodie with a hug. "Welcome to the big house."

"Sorry for imposing on you," Jodie said.

Jill waved off the apology and ushered them inside. "We're grateful for the company. And Izzy..." She closed the door to see her daughter had retreated back to hide behind the stair railing. "Apparently, Isabel is shy, but she really likes quizzing new people. Come on, honey. You remember Deputy Claire and Miss Jodie. And now her name is Sheriff Claire, so remember that."

Isabel marched out onto the porch, but her face remained unsure. "Hi, Sheriff Claire."

"Hi, Izzy."

To Jodie, she said, "What's your job?"

Jill looked horrified, but Jodie only laughed. "I fix cars."

"*Real* cars?" Isabel said, her worry evaporating.

"Yep. Cars, trucks, motorcycles, I do all of it."

Isabel turned without another word and ran up the stairs, lifting her knees as high as she could to take them two at a time.

"Uh-oh," Jill laughed. "You've done it now. These days she's really fascinated by what people do for a living. And she loves, loves, loves cars." She smoothed her hand over her hair and looked at them, their bags, and then toward the kitchen. "Have you eaten...?"

They confirmed they had. Claire said, "We'll do our best to stay out of your way while we're here."

Isabel came running downstairs and stopped in front of Jodie. She held up a small yellow Hot Wheels car cupped with both hands. When she spoke, she carefully formed each word. "Ford Tuh-ri-no Co-bwa," she said, then corrected herself. "Co-bra."

Jodie said, "A 1969, if I'm not mistaken. It's awesome."

"It's my favorite," Isabel whispered.

"Well, I'd really like to see the rest once I get settled in."

Isabel beamed, nodded, and ran back upstairs with the toy.

Jill said, "Well, I know how Jodie's going to be spending her stay with us. I hope you brought a book or something, Claire."

Claire had been dreading this moment. "Actually, I'm... I'm just dropping Jodie off. I'm heading back out."

"The hell you are," Jodie said, then looked to make sure Isabel hadn't returned. "Claire. You're not going after them."

Claire didn't waver. "I am."

Jill took a step back. "I have some papers to grade, so..."

Jodie waited until she was gone, then stepped closer to Claire. "No."

"I have to."

"You said you didn't want to relive what happened in Chicago," Jodie said. "Have you ever wondered what Elaine was going through while you were missing? I don't want to get word from Alex that she's pulled you out of a wrecked car. I don't want to lay awake tonight wondering if I'm never going to see you again."

Claire looked down at her feet. "If not me, who? Who is going to help those women? Who is going to stop Wyman from doing this over and over again?"

Jodie stepped back and turned away from her. "Go."

Claire sighed. "Jodie..."

"Just go." Her voice was defeated and sad, which was worse than anger would have been.

"I love you," Claire said.

"Yeah, I know."

Jodie didn't look at her as she headed up the stairs to go look at Isabel's cars. Claire waited until she heard the sound of the seven-year-old's voice before she let herself out of the house.

***

Claire walked back to their house, nearly a mile in blustery wind that occasionally peppered her face with ice crystals. It was a torturous walk, but it was one she felt she deserved. The street in front of her house was ridiculously crowded, with the fire engine parked on one side, the town's only remaining squad car on the other, and a tow truck parked sideways in the road with its warning lights flashing on their neighbor's houses. Yellow crime scene tape had been stretched between the mailbox and the fence's end post, blocking their driveway and the charred wreckage of her cruiser.

Alex saw her coming and came to meet her. "Are you like one of those dogs who instinctively wanders home if the gate is left unlocked?"

"Yeah, maybe. Are you going to take the car?"

"We were about to start loading it up. Why?"

"I just need it out of my way."

Alex looked at her and decided not to push it. "Give us about twenty minutes."

Claire nodded and went into the house. In a town where it was easy to walk pretty much everywhere, it was easy to get by with just Jodie's car and the squad car. But they had another vehicle, which they kept in a garage at the end of the driveway. She had to dig through their junk drawer to find the keys, but they were there. She knew the car would run because Jodie made it a point of pride to give the car a check-up every few months.

"I'd be a pretty shit mechanic if I had a brick sitting in my backyard," she said. "I know I wouldn't trust that mechanic to work on *my* car."

The warning beep of the tow truck echoed through the house. While the squad car was being loaded onto the bed, she went down the hall to retrieve some extra ammunition. She had no idea what she was going to face in the next few hours, but she wanted to be prepared. She passed a framed photo on the wall, the same photo she passed every day but had stopped noticing a long time ago, so she went back and made herself look at it.

Their wedding day, standing with the harbor behind them. Claire, looking above the camera with a pained look. Jodie, looking off to the left, caught mid-laugh at Claire's discomfort at posing for the picture. They were both in button-down shirts, but Jodie wore a bright blue bowtie with hers. She didn't remember who had taken the picture. Rucker, Randall, a few other cops, and some of Jodie's coworkers were all there, but she couldn't remember who had been the one to ask for an official picture.

"This is torture for you, isn't it?" Jodie had asked as she pressed up against Claire's left shoulder.

"The ends justify the means. I can handle it. As long as you're here." Claire paused. "But it's almost over, right?" Jodie laughed, and that's when the picture was taken.

Her phone buzzed in her pocket. She took it out and saw the first line of Jodie's text displayed on the screen. "I love you." Claire took a breath and then opened the full message. "It was petty and stupid of me not to say it, tonight of all nights, given what you're doing."

Jodie had definitely said it. She said it by being angry with her for not staying, by being scared and wanting her to be safe. She may not have said the words, but the feeling was definitely expressed in an unmistakable way.

"You were right to be angry," Claire wrote in a reply, "but I also don't believe I'm wrong. I'll be safe. I love you."

"I love you too," arrived within ten seconds of Claire sending the response.

She turned off the phone and slipped it into her pocket. A glance through the front window showed her that the driveway was clear, so she turned out the lights and locked up the house. Her feet crunched the snow as she crossed the lawn and pushed up the rusty garage door. Worktables were cluttered with junk and tools lined all three walls, but the majority of the space was filled by a tarp-covered car. She stared at the cloth and what she knew lay under it, what the car symbolized. She'd needed a car that wasn't traceable to her. She had no destination in mind beyond "away," distance, and every city she passed achieved that goal.

There were weeks when the car was her home. She'd slept in every seat of it, sometimes spent twenty-four hours straight behind the wheel, and for a time she'd been positive she would die in it.

Claire stepped into the gap on the driver's side, gripped the tarp, and slowly pulled it back. Dark blue chrome that gleamed even in the barely-perceptible light. She gathered the tarp in her arms and dumped it on the table, opened the door as far as she could, and slipped into the driver's seat. She wrapped her fingers around the cold leather of the steering wheel.

She was transported back in time, to Saxe, Texas. Oklahoma City. Road Ends, Montana. Shepherd, Washington. Crystal Springs, Nevada. She remembered men who held her prisoner, who put guns to her head, who threatened and hurt her, who tied her to the back of a car and dragged her through a desert. She lowered her head and closed her eyes. She flexed her fingers on the wheel. Starting the car would be waking up a side of herself she'd long ago put to bed.

It had always been safer to be someone else. To be Chloe Lassiter, Carmen Landry, Claire Lowe. Or Claire Curran.

She could hide. She could drive back to the mayor's residence, go upstairs, and watch Jodie play Hot Wheels with a seven year old. It sounded like paradise, honestly, even if she wasn't comparing it to this freezing car and the threat posed by a group of men who had already proven themselves capable of murder. She leaned forward and put her head on the wheel.

It didn't matter what name she used, she was still the same person she always was. She was the person who jumped into the fire to save someone else from burning. She took the keys out of her pocket and sat up straight as she slipped them into the ignition.

The Mustang roared to life.

CHAPTER NINE

CLAIRE DROVE out of town, passing the unmarked road to turn down Spence Alley. She wished she'd asked the woman at the post office how many people lived on this road, but it was too late now. She counted five mailboxes, but only two seemed to be in regular use. She wanted to cut her headlights but there was no way she'd be able to follow the road's bends without them. Eventually she reached a straight stretch with a house on either side. She drove past the houses to what seemed like a dead end and parked with the headlights shining on a stand of trees packed so closely together they almost formed a natural fence.

She got out and opened the trunk. She traded her Stetson for a knit cap, pulled on a thick dark coat, and checked to make sure her gun was loaded before slipping it into her holster.

"Hooze air," someone grunted from far too close to her.

She turned slowly and saw someone standing on the grass at the edge of the road. The trees had kept the snow here from being too thick, but she could still see a weaving trail of footprints leading back toward one of the houses. She couldn't make out any of his features, but thin hair stood out in a halo around his head. He looked hunched over, more like a tree stump than a human being.

"Said 'who's there,'" he repeated, and this time she was able to make out the words.

"Sheriff Curran, sir. I'm just parking here on official police business."

He said, "Sheriff? Of here? Sheriff here is an old man."

"We've had a few hectic days, sir. I'm just going to cross through the back of your property to hopefully catch them by surprise."

The man grunted. His head swiveled around, then snapped back to her. "Is your business 'bout them fellas moved in over yonder?"

"It may. Why?"

He turned without answering and shuffled back toward the house. "Buncha lousy noisy..." He grumbled, his voice fading quickly.

Claire watched him go, then shook her head and shut the trunk. She was halfway across the lawn when the old man came shuffling up alongside her.

"Hold your dang horses. Here."

She thought he was handing her a branch, but quickly realized it was a shotgun. "Sir, I can't take that."

"Y'oughta have one of yer own. I saw you with that little one, ain't gonna scare these boys with that." He gestured with it. "G'wan. Take it."

She finally relented. "Thank you. I'll return it when I come back to the car."

He was already walking back toward the house. "Bring it back empty, and you'll be doin' e'ry one of us a favor."

Claire waited until he was inside before she continued on her way.

The trees were tightly packed. She occasionally paused so she could use her phone's flashlight to get her bearings before she went on. Fortunately it was only a short trek between the two roads and it wasn't long before she could see by the light coming from Wyman's properties. She slowed her progress and sank down into a crouch, holding the borrowed rifle across her chest until she reached the tree line. She put her shoulder against a tree and eyed the layout.

Six houses, two on one side of the street with three on the other, and a larger house at the end of the road. She assumed that was the main house. Generators hummed loudly behind at least two houses where she could see lights, but she assumed they were all outfitted for power. Two cars and a white van were parked at the head of the road in an area which seemed to have been designated as the motor pool. Even at a distance she could tell one of the cars matched Jodie's description.

Voices rose from one of the houses. Claire risked moving closer, checking to make sure no one was outside before she trotted to take cover behind the nearest house. The shadows concealed her as she moved to the next house, one with light coming from the windows, but the voices were coming from farther away.

The voices were coming from the main house, and she was only separated from it by a wide empty stretch of snowy grass. Someone shouted, and he was far enough away that she risked stepping out into the open. She took long, loping strides and stopped herself just before impacting the side of the house, holding her breath, waiting to find out she'd been discovered. But the next raised voice she heard came from the other side of the house.

"It doesn't *matter* if she didn't see you! Do you think she'll chalk this up to an isolated incident? She's going to know exactly who did this."

"Den, you okayed kidnapping the wife. When that fell apart, we assumed you'd want to send the message another way."

"So you set her car on fire!" Dennis snapped. "Do you have any idea the sort of spotlight you've turned on us? My plan wasn't to kidnap the wife, you imbecile. We were going to drive her around and talk sense into her. I was going to convince her to convince this idiot sheriff to back off. Just a conversation! And if she was a little intimidated, then..." He sighed, but it sounded like a growl. "You... you morons got drunk and threw a Molotov cocktail into a *police car*."

"It wasn't technically a Molotov cocktail. It~"

"Do you *really* want to correct me right now, you piece of shit?"

Silence.

"So... s-so what, uh, what do you want to do now?"

"You assholes have backed me into a corner here. I could have talked us out of this. I could have worked things out the way I've worked it out a dozen times in other cities. Every cop has their price, but not if you antagonize them. Not if you make it personal. Now there's no amount of money that will make this bitch back off."

More silence. Claire inched further along the house, nearly to the corner to the backyard. There was too much light in the space to risk peeking, but she'd heard three distinct voices. With Lile and Packard in custody, that left one person unaccounted for. She couldn't make a move until she knew where he was, or where the women were. She didn't want some wild card who could turn this into a hostage situation.

"Look," said the one she'd decided to call Dopey for no real reason, "we all read about her. We all saw the news shit about the bank robbery and that fucking song. You think we could've bought her off? You really think there's a price this Lance bitch would take to look the other way? She's fucking John Wayne. Jane Wayne."

The other man, who she dubbed Bashful because he hadn't spoken much, said, "Tom Joad."

"The fuck?" Dennis grunted.

"It's... from a book..."

Dopey said, "My point is that maybe this is a good thing. All right? If you aren't gonna talk her into playing nice, maybe scaring her is the right way to go."

Dennis laughed low and quiet, almost a rumble. "All that stuff you mentioned. The song and the bank robbery. That might prove she can't be bought, but it *definitely* proves she's not the type to be scared away. All you've done, you stupid son of a bitch, is rattle the beehive."

The snow started to pick up, increasing from barely noticeable to a thick swirl. It occurred to Claire that, while it was very fortunate for her purposes, it was odd for the men to be having this conversation outside given the weather. The only plausible reason was that they didn't want someone in the house to overhear.

"I thought you said taking out the other sheriff was the wrong move."

"With Rucker, yeah! We had him right where we wanted him. *He* was old. *He* was used to coasting. He was perfect. Given enough pressure, he would have taken the money just to keep the peace. I just had to break him a little more."

Claire closed her eyes and rested her head against the wall. Callum Rucker would never have broken. When these bastards pushed him to that point, he'd chosen to take himself off the board. He made it her fight because he knew she was better equipped. His death was tragic, but now it was also heartbreakingly unnecessary. If he had moved a little faster, or been less secretive, he would have been off their radar entirely.

"Goddamn it, Ruck," she mouthed, the words existing as puffs of white smoke only she could see before they evaporated.

"~just her," Dopey was saying. "We're talking about her wife, too. And probably her friends in the department who would come after us just on principle."

Bashful said, "Are we prepared to do that? I mean... I mean, I know it's a small town..."

"He might have a point there, Den. We have two people in with them already..."

"Are you counting Teddy?" Dennis interrupted. "Because from what you yourself told me, he's going to have a hard time feeding himself. Forget about staging a coup."

Dopey said, "Okay, fine, but Georgie is reliable. He's in the actual building. He'd know about their numbers, their schedule, maybe even the layout of the building. He could give us some intel."

"If the cops ever let us talk to him alone."

Bashful said, "They'll have to eventually, if we aren't allowed to leave the room."

Dennis was silent. "You mean one of us get arrested on purpose."

Bashful said, "You said it yourself, she's pissed. It won't take much to make her pounce. One of us runs a stop sign, she'll find a reason to drag us in and throw us in a cell. She's going to want to make a point. I say... maybe we let her, you know? Give her a third prisoner, when all she'll really be doing is making a Trojan Horse."

"Is that from another fucking book?" Dopey grumbled.

"Shut up, Ryan."

Claire was disappointed to hear the man's real name. Dopey fit him so well.

The temperature seemed to have dropped drastically since she left the car. She flexed the fingers of one hand, then the other. The men were still talking, discussing the logistics of the Trojan Horse plan. Claire retreated back along the side of the house to the shining square of a window. She stood still and listened for any sounds coming from within before she risked stretching up to peek inside.

She looked directly into the face of a woman who was staring back at her.

They both froze. The woman was standing at a sink, her wet hands resting on the counter. The expression on her face indicated her mind had been wandering when Claire suddenly appeared in her line of sight. Her eyebrows were up, eyes wide enough to show whites all around the dark irises, and her mouth hung open in a thankfully silent O. Claire pressed a finger to her lips, hoping and praying the woman wouldn't scream out of instinct.

The woman looked toward the back door.

No, come on, don't.

She looked back and Claire and waved her away with both hands. When Claire didn't move, the woman mouthed, "Go!" in a way that changed her whole face. It was a plea: save yourself, run.

After checking to make sure the men were still talking, Claire pulled aside her jacket. The kitchen light glinted off her badge. The woman's eyes widened again. She mouthed: "Claire Lance?"

Claire nodded. This woman was obviously why they were having the conversation outside. They didn't want her to overhear the plan. The only question was if she was a prisoner or somehow willingly part of the group. But then why would she be trying to send Claire away? She was dressed in a wool sweater, the sleeves pushed up past the elbows, and she seemed to be wearing makeup. She didn't look like a prisoner. But she had no idea what a prisoner in this context might look like.

She pointed at the woman and gestured toward the front of the house. The woman shook her head in violent refusal. Claire made a "come with me" motion but the woman's head continued rocking side to side. She backed away from the sink.

Dennis was saying, "~volunteer? Because I'm not going to get locked up. Are you, Ryan? How about you, Tim? I don't see either of you being great spies."

The woman had left the sink but was coming back when Claire looked again. She had gotten a bottle of ketchup from the fridge and smeared some on two fingers. She picked up one of the clean plates and wrote on it. Claire couldn't help smiling; she kind of loved this lady. She finished writing and held up the plate.

I'M OK. GO!!!

Claire desperately didn't want to leave this woman behind, but she didn't see an alternative short of abducting her. She nodded and the woman's shoulders slumped with relief. She plunged the plate into the water, obliterating the message with a sweep of her hand. Claire retreated back into the shadows, this time moving toward the front of the house. The voices from the backyard were quieter but still clear enough to understand given the night's silence.

"Jesse will volunteer if we tell him he can make a cop look like an idiot," she heard Ryan say.

She was at the front corner of the house when she heard a door close. She froze and pressed tight against the side of the house as a man - Jesse, she presumed - walked out of the nearest house. She recognized him from Rucker's photos; he was the man with a prison tattoo on his neck. He balanced a covered tray on one hand while he locked the door behind him with the other. He grabbed the knob and gave it a violent shake before he turned toward the main house.

Claire held her breath. There was nothing at all between them, no cover beyond the shadows and his own lack of attention. He looked up at the tumbling snow, stuck out his tongue like a child, then looked down to watch his step so he wouldn't slip on the ice. Claire tracked him with her eyes, keeping the shotgun still despite every muscle telling her to bring it up into position. But movement would catch his eye, and at the moment she was essentially invisible.

He swayed on his feet and hummed under his breath, then moved out of her view. She heard a door open and close. She waited a beat to make sure he'd gone inside before poking her head around the corner to make sure. When she saw the porch was empty, she darted across the open space to the house he'd left. It was one of the houses hooked up to a generator, which was humming noisily on the north side of the house. She tried the knob knowing it was pointless, then went around to the other side.

She'd seen a lot of houses like this since coming to the island. They were built out of necessity and rarely up to any sort of code. It was most likely only a couple of rooms with thin walls. The windows were all secured and weatherproofed, which would have impressed her if it didn't get in the way of her rescue attempt.

The back door was even worse. She didn't know if it was locked or if it was so warped in the frame that opening it was impossible, but either way she couldn't get it to budge.

She had just stepped away from the door when she heard a quiet knock on the other side. She stopped, came closer, and returned the knock: two taps, pause, two taps.

She was answered almost immediately: Tap-tap-tap. Tap. Tap. Tap. Tap-tap-tap.

SOS.

Claire only knew the basics of Morse code, nowhere near enough to have a conversation. She doubted whoever was on the other side of the door knew more than what had already been sent. She stepped close enough to the back door that she could feel the cold emanating from it against her cheek.

"Can you hear me?"

"Yes."

"My name is Claire Curran. I'm the sheriff. I'm going to get you out of there, but I need to know how many of you there are."

There was a pause. "Only four now." Her voice was accented, but they were speaking too quietly for her to narrow it down. "One of us is in the other house. With the men."

"Five total?"

"Yes."

"I'm going to do everything I can to get you out of here. I need you to hold tight, okay?"

Silence. Then, "Please, hurry."

"What's your name?"

"Tereza."

Claire said, "I'll be back, Tereza, you have my word." She knocked twice on the door and stepped back until she could see the other house. Five hostages and four angry men with guns who had just decided she was too much trouble to keep alive. It killed her to leave, just the thought made her want to storm the main house and take her chances, but that would result in a bloodbath for both sides. The snow had started falling faster, and the temperature had taken another dip. Even if everything went perfectly and she arrested all four men, there was a chance she'd be stuck here with them. She didn't like those odds.

She knew what she was up against. She had names and she knew how their home base was situated. It would have to do for now.

With one last look at the house where the five women were being held, Claire reluctantly retreated into the woods.

When she got back to the other clearing, one of the houses had a light shining on the porch. The hunched old man was sitting in what looked like a homemade chair.

"I didn't hear you use that," he said, nodding at the shotgun, "but if you did, you can just toss it back into the woods and leave it there."

"It didn't come to that." She stepped onto the porch and held the weapon out to him. "Thank you for the loan."

He made a noise that may have just been caused by the effort of leaning forward to take it from her. He stood and looked her over.

"You want to know more about them folks? Already told it to the other fella, but if he's really gone, I guess you might oughta hear it, too."

Claire said, "I would definitely appreciate that, sir, if you have the time."

"Sir," he snorted. He had already turned and was moving through the front door. "Guy."

"Pardon?"

"Guy, Guy." He twisted at the waist and thumped a hand against his chest. "My name. Call me Guy. None of that 'sir' stuff."

Claire followed him inside. "Oh. I apologize." Guy had always seemed like an odd name to her. She'd never known any women named Lady. "I'm Claire."

Another noise from the man, as if this was inconsequential information. He walked past a seating area with an armchair and a loveseat, into a kitchenette. He turned on a hot plate and began rearranging items on the counter. The house was surprisingly cozy and warm given the isolated location. A door at the back of the room led into what looked like a small sleeping area. Standing inside, with a space heater humming a few feet away, she realized how absolutely frozen she was.

"Was nice and peaceful up here. Then they showed up. About a year ago. Generators running at all hours. Hum, hum, hum. You hear it?"

"I heard it when I was over there. Can't really hear it now, though."

"I can hear it. Believe me, I can. All us on this road can hear it. All hours of the night," he repeated. "Joseph went over there to talk to 'em about it. Came back with a shiner and a limp. Said the guy in charge warned him that the next one of us who went over there wouldn't come back." He looked at her. "What the hell are you doing? Sit down. We're having a conversation."

"Right." She chose the loveseat over the chair. "So none of you have gone over there since?"

"We want peace and quiet, not a feud. Joey seemed pretty damn convinced they meant business. So we just put up with it. But we kept an eye on everything happening. And when Cal showed up, hell, we were more'n willing to talk his ear off and let him take the risk." He stopped what he was doing and stared at a spot on the wall. "He, ah... he was..."

Claire said, "I know."

"Huh." He shook his head and went back to preparing a drink. "Well. At least we were right about them being a real threat. I guess that's something. Good thing we didn't press our luck or we might all have..." He sighed. "I'm sorry. About Cal."

She was shuddering now, but trying not to show it. "I want to finish what he started. Anything you can tell me about these guys would be a great help."

Guy poured a cup of coffee and brought it to her. She wrapped her hands around it, sighing at the warmth, and thanked him as he folded himself into the chair.

"Six guys. The weasel-face one seems to be in charge. Smile so big but it don't show his teeth, little eyes, limp hair. Could be handsome but looks like he just crawled out of a sewer."

"That would be Dennis Wyman."

Guy sneered. "Dunno names. They showed up here, just took those houses just 'cause they were empty. Like they was owed, or something." He sniffed and looked out the window, watching the snow fall. "After what happened with Joey, we thought maybe peace. Ignore the fact they stole that whole street and try to be good neighbors. Drew's wife Alice went over with a casserole. Figured six men living alone might like a homecooked meal. One of the jackasses took the pan from her and dumped it out right on the grass. Told her not to bother them anymore." He huffed and shook his head. "I don't care who you are, food's food. And Alice makes a damn fine casserole. Not just mean for meanness sake, but wasteful."

He shifted uncomfortably. Claire waited.

"Then the ladies started showing up. Not sure when the first group showed, but eventually we realized they was over there."

"You 'realized'?" Claire said.

He turned his hard gaze on her. "We kept tabs on 'em. Bunch of bastards like that squat next door, wouldn't you do the same?"

"Absolutely I would," Claire confirmed.

"Drew saw a bunch of women get out of a truck. Said they was all dressed the same, all looked like whipped pups. They got marched into one of those houses over there. Every now and then, we see one of the ladies get in a truck with one of the guys and they..." He waved a trembling hand in an 'away' gesture. "We don't see the women after they leave."

Claire said, "Do you have any idea where they women come from?"

"They just show up. Hard to say how many there are... they leave one at a time, pretty regular... but then three or four more show up. One of the fellas goes out in a truck, usually at night, and comes back with new ladies. I doubt there's ever more than ten there." He looked at Claire. "So what do you plan to do about all this?"

"Whatever I can," Claire said. "I've stopped bad men before. I can do it again."

Guy stared at her as if he was reading a resume on her face. "They'll fight back."

"They usually do."

"If there's anything you need to do where that," he pointed at her badge, "gets in the way, come over here and let us know. I don't want to incriminate nobody for nothing. But if hands gotta get dirty, it probably washes off better from ours than from police's."

Claire said, "I hope it won't come to that, but thanks." She finished the coffee and put the cup down on the table. "Thank you for the drink. And the gun. And for filling me in about your neighbors."

"Don't thank me. Just get to work. What did you say your name was again?"

"Curran. Claire Curran."

He nodded and pushed up out of his chair. He extended a hand to her. The skin felt like sandpaper when she gripped it.

"Good luck, Sheriff Curran."

She nodded and left the house, tucking her chin into the collar of her coat as she headed down the stairs. She had to brush a layer of snow off the windows of her car before she got in. When she turned the car around to leave, she saw Guy was still standing on the porch to watch her go. She lifted her hand, and he threw what might have been a salute before he went back inside. The porch light clicked off in his wake, and the house was thrown back into deep shadows.

On the drive back into town, she saw the snow was starting to accumulate on streets and buildings. From the mayor's property she could see all the way down Spring Street to the harbor, and every storefront looked like it belonged on a Christmas card. She rolled down the window, entered the gate code Patricia had given her that afternoon, and rolled through. She let the car idle as the gate rolled shut behind her, then got out and made sure it was secured before she drove the rest of the way up to the front door.

The house was silent, dark except for one room at the back of the ground floor. She took off her jacket, hat, and boots and hung them up to dry next to the door. A silhouette blocked the light coming from the back room, and it took Claire a moment to recognize Mayor Hood-Colby out of context. She was in white silk pajamas, her hair down, and she was wearing a pair of thick glasses. She looked a foot shorter than usual, and Claire wondered if that was because she was barefoot or just because she wasn't in her office at City Hall.

"How'd everything go?" she whispered.

Claire shrugged and shook her head. "Hard to tell. Maybe productive."

"Here's hoping." She nodded at the stairs. "You and Jodie are in the first room at the top of the stairs. It used to be our son's room, so don't be surprised when you wake up and find a bunch of baseball stuff on the walls."

"I'll brace myself. But considering how we left things, Jodie might expect me to take the couch."

Patricia said, "Jill told me there was a disagreement. Can I offer you some marital advice?"

"Sure."

"Offer to take the couch if she needs the space. But never, ever assume it's what she wants. Have the conversation."

Claire nodded. "Thanks, Mayor."

"Patricia. In my house, after midnight, in my pajamas, you can call me Patricia."

"Okay. Goodnight."

"Goodnight, Claire."

Claire went upstairs, stepping on the balls of her feet to minimize the sound. The bedroom door was open a crack and she slipped inside. Jodie was lying on top of the covers with her hands folded on her stomach. She didn't move when Claire closed the door behind her.

"I know you're awake."

Jodie said, "No, I'm not. I passed out hours ago and I've been sleeping like a baby."

Claire finished undressing, draping her uniform over a chair before she lay down next to Jodie.

"Thank you for sending the text."

Jodie rolled onto her side so they were facing each other. "We were both sort of wrong." She touched Claire's cheek and a line appeared between her eyebrows. "Claire, you're *freezing*."

"I—"

"Shh." She scooted closer and wrapped her arms around Claire, squeezing her tightly. "I know who you are. You're the woman who robbed a bank to keep me from becoming a bank robber. You do stupid things sometimes. But you're always doing the right thing, without worrying about the consequences. But you know who I am, too. I'm the woman who is always going to be scared and worried that you'll get hurt. We have to take that with everything else we love about each other. I can do that."

"I can, too," Claire said.

Jodie pulled the blanket tighter around them. "Let me warm you up." She put her head down on Claire's chest. "This is a really nice house."

"It is."

"You should run for mayor so we can have it."

Claire smiled. "You want it, you run for mayor."

"No, you."

"No, you."

"No," Jodie murmured.

Claire stroked Jodie's hair and drifted off.

CHAPTER TEN

THE AIR was scorching, and she was the woman she used to be. She was Lance again.

Lance was stripped down to a tank top, but that only let the sun burn her skin directly. Sweat poured from her, stinging her eyes. She felt like she was literally being cooked alive. The car behind her also radiated heat. She shielded her eyes from the offending sun. At the end of the road, she saw a shimmer that might be a town.

Lance remembered that town. She remembered this road. The heat had snapped her out of the zombified state she'd existed in since Elaine's death, forcing her to acknowledge she could die if she didn't take action. She'd been eating only when she was starving. She mostly drank beer, unconcerned about driving under the influence. She did everything in a trance anyway, so what was a little fog of alcohol?

Lance started walking. Horses ran by, one herd on either side of the road, their hooves thundering without kicking up any sand. They were the horses from Kelsey and Andrea's ranch, in Montana.

This was the road where she started on the path of becoming who she was now. She was a shell of a woman with nothing to live for, no hope.

There was another figure on the road, walking toward her, wearing full racing gear despite the heat. She was moving fast, swinging her arms, helmeted head held high.

Lance held out a hand to her.

The Race Car Driver lifted one hand with the middle finger extended. She stepped around Lance and kept walking.

Lance turned to face her. "Calico!"

The Race Car Driver stopped.

Lance stared at her back. Her heart pounded. She thought about walking on, back into the bar. The men with guns who would hold her hostage in an Oklahoma hotel room. The man in Montana who threatened awful things, who hurt people to get his way. The bank robbery. The hunters in Alaska she'd only evaded by sheer, dumb luck. The crooked cops who had come so damn close to killing her. She knew she would do it all again, face them all again if she needed to. She would risk bullets, blades, beatings, whatever they could dole out.

"Jodie."

The scariest thing she'd done in all her years on the road had been falling for Jodie Curran. She made herself vulnerable to hurt. She'd put Jodie in danger just being near her, and yet she couldn't stay away. Falling in love was selfish and she should have run away as soon as she felt the first stirrings. But she couldn't.

Jodie should have run, too. God, why hadn't she run away? A fugitive, a target for bad men, someone who couldn't resist stepping in front of speeding buses. Lance had been such a bad choice. But Jodie stayed. Jodie waited for her.

Lance walked to the Race Car Driver. They were different people now. They left Lance and Calico behind.

They were Jodie and Claire Curran of Squire's Isle.

Claire took off the Race Car Driver's helmet. It was Jodie as she looked now, not as she had looked all those years ago in Shepherd, Washington. Laugh lines, gray hairs at the temple, a calmness in her eyes where there'd once been recklessness. Claire knew her face had changed, too. She'd seen it in the mirror.

"I don't have to walk this road anymore," she said.

Jodie smiled and brushed the hair out of Claire's face. "Claire Lance, you've been walking this road your whole life. Why would you stop now, when people still need you?"

Claire looked to the left and saw a house surrounded by snow, despite the fact her skin was still burning in the sun.

Tereza.

Four other women whose names she didn't know, but who had probably been told her name by now. She existed in their minds as hope, as potential for freedom.

"It could kill me."

"Not doing it could kill you, too. Make you someone else. Someone I couldn't be in love with."

Claire looked at Jodie, whose face was oddly shadowed. She was lying down, Claire realized. They both were, and the room was dark. She was cold despite the blanket. She blinked at Jodie.

"What?" Jodie said.

"What?"

"You..." Jodie narrowed her eyes. "Were you talking in your sleep?"

Claire said, "I might have been..."

Jodie smiled. "I should have known. You called me Calico."

"It's a good nickname." She leaned close and kissed Jodie by one eye.

"The woman I fell in love with risked having her face on television to protect me. I'm scared as all hell. It's taking everything in my being to not kidnap you, take you to Hawaii, and start a new life as a coconut farmer. But I know a couple of things for certain. One, you're you. Whatever name you use, you've always been the white knight. Asking you to change that would be like banning me from being around cars. It might happen, but I wouldn't be the same person."

"Probably true."

"Two," Jodie said, "these guys aren't going to just stop and go away. Women are going to get hurt. Women are getting hurt right now. Someone has to stop that. If it's not you, who else is going to do it?"

Claire nodded.

"Three... I love you. That might have been covered in number one. I'm tired. But it deserves to be restated."

"I love you, too. And if the worst does happen, I want you to know that meeting you, falling in love with you, getting to build this life with you, has been the scariest thing I've ever done. And it's the thing I'm proudest of."

Jodie pressed her lips to the corner of Claire's mouth, then lifted her head to whisper in Claire's ear.

"Then *fight for it*, Lance."

Claire wrapped her arms around Jodie so she wouldn't go back to her side of the bed. Jodie settled on top of her. She had no idea how much time they had until morning, but she was willing to bet she could still get a few quality hours of sleep. She planned to spend as much of it as possible with Jodie in her arms.

CHAPTER ELEVEN

CLAIRE ASSUMED she would be the first one awake when she slipped out of bed at five-thirty. She tucked the blankets tight around Jodie's shoulders and kissed her forehead.

"Has it been at least four hours?" Jodie murmured.

"Maybe," Claire said.

Jodie pressed her lips together, either too tired to argue or deciding it was pointless. "Try again tonight."

"Promise." She kissed Jodie again and left the bedroom.

She stood on the landing and took a moment to get a feel for the house. She'd never been there before, and it was odd trying to acclimate herself this early in the morning. While she stood there, she heard music coming from a room downstairs. She followed the sound downstairs and took the opportunity to admire the house.

She'd never been in the mayor's residence, but given its stately position on its own acre of land at the edge of town, she'd expected a mansion. It *was* large, and some of the furniture was gaudy and ostentatious, but it was easy to tell what had come with the house and what Patricia and Jill actually chose and used. Toys and books were scattered here and there, evidence of the child in residence. She followed the music through the dining room and recognized the string section just before she knocked on the office door.

"Did she have a bad dream?" Patricia asked without looking up.

Claire leaned into the doorway. "Sorry. It's me."

"Oh." She took off her glasses. "I thought you were..."

Patricia looked toward the device which was still playing music next to her laptop. "*...ending this dance. If you need to find me, I'm on the road with*

Lance."

"Shit, I'm sorry." She poked quickly at the screen to silence it.

"Don't be," Claire said. "It's a great song. Can I come in?"

"Of course." Patricia was wearing a T-shirt so faded the words that had once been written on it were impossible to read. Her hair was down and loose on her shoulders as if she'd just jumped out of bed and run downstairs. "I was just dealing with the storm."

Claire looked past her out the window. The side lawn of the house was a single solid wave of white, and flurries were still swirling.

"Bad?" she asked.

"Everything's shut down," Patricia said. "I was seeing if we could get some snowplows out, but it's not looking very likely until at least this afternoon."

"Damn."

Patricia said, "How did things go last night?"

"I learned a lot," Claire said, "but I wish I didn't have to wait for the weather to clear before I could move on it. I guess it's a blessing in disguise, since it means Wyman can't move the women to the mainland until the ferry is back in service."

"I hate the idea of these assholes setting up camp on my island. I hate thinking they've been here for so long. The number of women who have been held hostage here..." She angrily shook her head, stopping herself before she got carried away.

Claire said, "It happened on my watch, too. Rucker was the only one who knew about it, and he felt powerless to do anything. That's the whole reason he was stepping aside to let me take over."

"Whatever you need, as long as this takes, it's yours."

"Do you know of anywhere we can keep these guys if I do manage to arrest them? At the moment our only option is splitting them up in the cells, but I don't like the idea of them being able to talk with each other."

"Sure. The old isolation cells."

"That sounds ominous."

Patricia smiled. "Well, they *are* in a basement at the end of a dark hallway. It's in the courthouse. Back in the sixties before there was a separate police station, people were kept there while they awaited trial. Single rooms with reinforced doors. Basically solitary confinement. Right now they're filled with office equipment, but I can call someone and have it all moved just in case we need them."

"How secure are the rooms?"

"Very. You could probably keep watch on all the doors with one deputy."

"About that," Claire said. "I could use a few more deputies. We have the volunteers, but if we can put them in actual uniforms... It would most likely only be necessary for a little while, until this whole thing blows over..."

Patricia was already nodding. "Like seasonal work. I'll find it in the budget."

"Thank you. I was going to thank you for your hospitality by starting breakfast. Anything I should know?"

"Coffeemaker by the oven is for the house. Make yours in that. The one by the sink is for Jill. Don't touch it."

"You have two coffeemakers?"

Patricia shrugged, sighed, and slumped back in her chair. "She does weird stuff to it. She explained it to me a dozen times but I finally just decided we should retreat to separate counters. She'll come down and make it herself. She prefers it that way."

"She doesn't mind you being down here at five in the morning?"

"She knows it's sometimes necessary. And it's not every day. We keep strange hours. Some nights she's still up grading papers when I go to bed. And then adhering to whatever schedule Isabel needs us to keep. We make it work." She smiled. "Jodie knows, Claire. She may get mad at you for running out at all hours, she may yell at you for waking up too early or not getting enough sleep, but she knows you're doing what needs to be done. She's just doing her part to keep you grounded."

"Sometimes I worry I make it too hard on her."

Patricia shrugged. "So make it easier when you can. And make it up to her when you can't. I know you do what you can, but there's no such thing as too much. Showing appreciation goes a really long way."

"I'll keep that in mind. Thanks, Patricia."

"Sure. Oh... she also volunteered you for chef duties to pay for your room. Use whatever you find in the pantry."

Claire laughed and saluted. "Will do. Coffeemaker by the oven...?"

"Yes."

"Got it."

Her smile faded as she went through the dark, cold house to the kitchen. The house with Tereza and the other women had a generator, and she'd seen Jesse leave with what looked like a tray of dirty dishes. Hopefully they were warm and being taken care of. If Wyman intended to sell the women, it would be in his best interest to make sure they stayed healthy. It was a disgusting thought, but it was the only thing bringing her any kind of comfort about the situation. If she couldn't hold onto that, she might be tempted to build a pair of snowshoes and trek up there on foot.

Claire was in the middle of making breakfast when a Tasmanian devil of energy rushed into the kitchen. Isabel, still in her pajamas, stopped short when she realized the woman at the stove wasn't her mother. Her body went stiff, eyes wide and confused, blinking behind her uncombed bangs.

Fortunately, Jill was right behind her. "Izzy, you remember Sheriff

Claire. She's staying with us."

"Oh yeah! Jodie! Is she here?"

"She's still asleep," Claire said.

"Can—"

"No," Jill said, interrupting the request. "You're going to help me make your breakfast. Then you're going to take a bath, and get dressed, and then we'll ask Jodie if she wants to play. Okay?"

Isabel agreed to the terms and went into the pantry. Jill joined Claire at the stove.

"Did you sleep okay?"

Claire nodded and gestured at the pan. "Jodie told me about making me your chef. I didn't know if Isabel had any restrictions..."

Jill shook her head. "No, all of this looks fine. She likes to choose her own banana, though. It can't be too yellow but it definitely can't be green. It's a very delicate dance." She snuck a glance at her coffeepot next to the sink. "I guess Trish told you I'm a dictator about my coffee."

"She mentioned something about that pot being off-limits, yeah."

"She says I do weird stuff to it. I make it *good*. You can have a cup if you want."

Claire could tell when an offer was insincere. "Thanks, but I've already had a cup of Patricia's swill. Tastes fine to me."

"Heathens," Jill muttered as she began filling her machine.

Isabel came out of the pantry with a not-too-yellow but definitely-not-green banana like a scepter. The adults watched her victory march out of the dining room before they spoke again.

"I told her she can watch cartoons on the iPad with breakfast since we're snowed in. So! I don't know, um, what you're allowed to tell me about an ongoing case. But Patricia implied it was pretty bad. Do we have any reason to worry about the people you're after coming here?"

Claire shook her head. "I don't think so. They'd need to know we were here to begin with, and the only people who know that are in this house. And Chief Crawford, but I don't think she'd tell anyone."

"Alex is trustworthy," Jill agreed.

Jodie came into the kitchen, hair tangled and still in her pajamas. "Coffee...?"

Jill poured her a cup. "I'm surprised you were able to escape Isabel. You're her new favorite thing."

"I asked if I could get a cup of coffee before I joined her to watch something called *Buddy Thunderstruck*. Cartoon?"

"Stop motion. Trucks. With a... dog or a rat or something, I'm not sure what he is."

Jodie raised an eyebrow. "Ooh, okay, I might not hate that." She smiled at Claire and leaned in to kiss her. "Good morning."

"Morning, pretty," Claire said.

To Jill, Jodie said, "I was thinking, if it's okay with you and Patricia, later today I could take Isabel out into the garage and show her around one of your cars. I won't take anything apart, but I can show her how the engine works."

"Oh, boy," Jill said. "You'd really be her favorite then. As long as it's not an imposition to you."

"We're stuck here anyway," Jodie said. "I'd be happy to educate her a little. I just wanted to be sure it was okay with you, because she might get a little messy."

Jill waved her hand. "By all means. We don't mind a little grease if it adds to her education. Thank you."

Jodie lifted her coffee to Jill in thanks, kissed Claire's cheek, and headed out of the kitchen. "I better go see this truck show. Call me when breakfast is ready?"

Claire promised she would.

When they were alone again, Jill said, "I don't like the idea of these people being on the same island as my little girl. Or my students. Hell, with *me*. But if they really are as dangerous as you say, maybe it would be better to wait until the weather clears and call in some bigger guns. The feds, or whoever is the next up the ladder."

Claire didn't want to tell her about Wyman's decision to go on the offensive, but she also didn't want to leave their family unprepared if his goons did show up at the house.

"We can't wait. They know who I am, and they know most of what I've figured out. They're going to come after me regardless. I have to be ready for whatever they pull next. I've already got two of them in custody. Only four left."

"Yeah, but you have to take them all out to win. They only have to take you out. Those are lousy odds, Claire."

"I've made a life out of beating odds like that," Claire said. "I escaped from police custody, eluded a federal agent with a personal vendetta against me, then managed to stay free for five years until my innocence was proven. But there is one big difference between all those bad men I stopped when I was on the road and what's happening now."

"What's that?"

"All those times, in Texas or Washington or Nevada, I was the new arrival. I came into town and found a problem waiting to be solved."

She took a sip of her coffee.

"These guys are on my turf."

***

"This is an extraordinarily bad plan."

"Because it will fail?" Claire asked.

Jodie thought for a second. "No, not necessarily. Any plan has the potential to fail, so who knows, but in terms of sheer recklessness... bad plan."

Claire zipped up the hoodie which made up her first layer of warmth. "We have the home court advantage. We can use that to beat these guys. We can use our knowledge of the island and its people to get the upper hand. Wyman won't be expecting anyone to show up today, which means he'll have his guard all the way down."

"Because he has a whit of common sense," Jodie muttered.

"This might be our best chance to catch him off-guard. He thinks we're on the defensive. I'm going to prove him wrong."

Patricia crossed her arms over her chest. "Run it by me again, please?"

"This is our town," Claire said, "so we have access to information he doesn't. Like, for instance, the fact that Joseph Hogan has a snowmobile that can get me up to Spence Alley. As far as they know, it will be impossible for anyone to get out there, so they won't be on high alert. So I'll hike over to Hogan's place~"

"In single-digit cold," Jodie pointed out, "with the wind blowing twenty miles an hour in your face the whole way."

"I'll bundle up," Claire said. "The main reason I couldn't stay longer last night is because I wasn't adequately prepared for the weather. I ran off without a plan. This time I have a plan. Stupid though it may be."

"Oh it definitely is," Jodie said.

Patricia looked between them, then looked at Jill. Her wife picked up on the signal.

"Trish, let's go see if we have warmer gloves for her..."

"Sure, that sounds like a two-person job," Patricia said, pushing away from the counter.

On their way out of the room, Jill whispered, "Sorry, I couldn't think of anything else..."

Claire waited until she heard them on the stairs before she spoke. "I can stay. I can call it off, try to forget it until we have a better plan."

"You're making me choose between what I want and the safety of five women who are in danger, Claire. Of course I want you to stay. Of course you have to go. I feel like shit for being angry." She pressed the heel of her hand against her eye. "But that's not your problem, and it's wrong of me to take it out on you."

Claire came closer and pulled Jodie into a hug. "It was easier when I was just running blind into danger. I didn't have to worry about someone at home."

"Do you wish it was still like that?"

Claire stepped back and looked at her. "When have you ever known me to prefer the easy way?"

Jodie smiled and pressed a kiss to Claire's lips. "Please don't ever get sick of me being upset about shit like this."

"As long as you don't ever stop feeling selfish about me," Claire said.

"Deal."

Patricia came back into the kitchen, her return suspiciously well-timed to the end of the argument, and presented Claire with a pair of thick gloves and a ski mask.

"Finish going over your plan," Patricia said. "What do you intend to do once you're up there?"

"Surveillance. I want to see how they act when they think no one's around."

Patricia said, "Won't they hear your snowmobile coming from a mile away? It's dead quiet out there, and I imagine the sound travels even better outside of town."

"One thing I did learn last night is that they have big generators running behind at least two of the houses. I doubt they'll hear much of anything over that."

"So you just get up there and stalk them?"

Claire shrugged. "We'll see what I can do once I'm up there. If I see an opening, I'll break into the house where the women are being held and get them out. I spoke to someone who lives on the next road over. I'm sure he'd be willing to give them shelter once they're out. Getting them to safety takes away Wyman's leverage. Then all bets will be off."

Patricia said, "I talked to Tobias, who is holding down the fort at City Hall today. We got the isolation rooms emptied out. They're ready if you want to start filling them up."

"Good to know." She touched Jodie's arm and squeezed. "I should head out. I don't know for sure how long it'll take me to walk to Hogan's house."

Patricia said, "It's just under a mile, but given the conditions..."

Claire nodded. "I'll take it nice and slow."

She went to the door and finished putting on her armor: a heavy jacket on top of the hoodie, then a North Face jacket on top of that. Gloves, a scarf tucked into the collar of her coat, and the ski mask pulled down over her face and tucked carefully into her shirt. Jodie also gave her a pair of sunglasses that didn't provide quite as much cover as goggles would, but they would be better than nothing.

"My knight in puffy armor," Jodie said, patting Claire's padded shoulders. "Go get 'em, killer."

Claire kissed Jodie, which amounted to pressing a layer of cotton against her cheek, and opened the door to head out into the snow.

***

Always listen to your wife, Claire thought as another gale of wind shoved her back a step. *Rule one of marriage and you blew it.*

The wind was unbelievable. She took a moment at the edge of the mayor's property to rethink her plan, wondering if it was a suicide mission. Even with all the layers she had on, the cold was stunning. The snow was almost to her knees where it had blown up against the property walls. It would be lower outside, but even then it would be above her ankles. She had made it this far, and she wouldn't retreat. It was eight-tenths of a mile to Hogan's house. Once she made it there, the rest of the trip would be simple. Eight-tenths of a mile was nothing. She would have killed for eight-tenths of a mile when she was on house arrest. It was barely considered exercise under normal conditions.

She looked out at the field of white. The snow was thick enough that it was hard to tell the difference between the sidewalk and the road.

"Not exactly normal conditions," she said, her voice muffled by the mask.

She pushed off and began marching, lifting her knees high to clear the dunes. She put her body on autopilot, one foot in front of the other, and let her mind focus on other things.

"Cabin fever?"

"Sure," Claire said, pushing away from the window. "That sounds better than house arrest."

Jodie put down her book and held out one arm to gesture her over. "Want to talk about it?"

Claire joined her on the couch, folding herself so her head was on Jodie's chest. "I know this is the absolute best-case scenario. I could be in prison right now. And my glorious thousand yard radius is extremely generous. I can get all the way to the corner store if I don't go to the cooler in the back. But it still sucks."

"I know, baby." Jodie kissed her hair. "Just a few more months, and then we can go wherever we want."

"We," Claire said. "You're not stuck here. You can go wherever you want right now."

Jodie said, "No. That ankle bracelet gives you a thousand yard radius, but I have a two-hundred yard radius from you. Any farther and I start to get all twitchy."

Claire lifted her head and kissed Jodie's neck. "You deserve better than being tethered to a woman who can't even get on a train."

"Trains are overrated."

The end of the block seemed like a good place to stop and take a breath. Not too much of a break. If she stopped long enough to sweat, to lose her momentum, she risked just shuddering and giving up. She didn't know how far she'd come, didn't want to think about how far she had to go. She grunted and pulled her foot out of the snow, planted it a little farther down the path, and continued her trek.

"I want to be Claire Curran."

"You tell people to call you Lance. It's literally the only thing I've ever heard some people call you. The woman who lived next to us in Chicago didn't even know your name was Claire!"

"I know. And now it's so much more than a name. It feels like it's not mine anymore. It belongs to that woman on the news, or the woman in the song. It's a character."

"It's you. You're the woman on the news."

"Jodie…" She took her girlfriend's hands, squeezed. "I spent my life as Lance. But that part of my life is done, and I want to start a new chapter. With you. I want people to know who saved me. I want to take your name."

"To hide?"

"No. Because these days, it feels more like me than Lance does. Claire Curran."

Jodie smiled. "It does have a certain ring to it… But if you take my name, does that mean we'd be married?"

"Do you want me to do the whole knee thing?"

"Not right now. And I don't need a ring. But I'd like a little ceremony when the time comes."

"I'll see what I can come up with."

She heard it before she saw it. Up ahead, like a mirage, a snowmobile swept around the corner and buzzed toward her. She stopped and stared as it approached and slowed to a stop right next to her. Joe 'Hoagie' Hogan, the second most popular disc-jockey on the island, pushed up his ski goggles and tugged down his mask to reveal a bright smile. His cheeks and the tip of his nose were bright red, and tufts of his shaggy white hair poked out from under his cap.

"Hey, Sheriff!"

"Mr. Hogan, we agreed I'd come to you."

He slung himself off the snowmobile. "I know what we agreed, but then I got to thinking. Why the hell am I making you come all the way to my place on foot when I could come to you and just have you drop me off at home before you go do whatever you have to do?"

"I…" Claire blinked. "It seemed easier this way."

Hogan raised an eyebrow. "Really? You want to finish this walk just to avoid a little backtracking?"

"It's not fair asking you to come out in this weather if I could just—"

He held up a hand. "Look, Mayor Hood-Colby didn't tell me exactly what's going on. But we have one sheriff in the ground and the new one is heading out on some top-secret mission in the middle of a blizzard. Whatever's going on, if my sledge can help, I'm willing to be a little inconvenienced. This is a small town, Sheriff Curran. We help each other."

Claire nodded slowly, ashamed of herself. "You think I'd have figured that out by now. I was just bragging about how well I knew this place, and I forgot the most important part of it. Thank you, Mr. Hogan."

"Hoagie. I insist. Now let's go, it's colder than shit out here and I want to get home before I freeze off my toes-ies."

Claire got into the snowmobile and Hoagie climbed on behind her. She was very much not a fan of that, but she had to admit it was better than finishing her walk. Fortunately there were handles to either side of his seat that he could hold onto instead of gripping her waist.

"Why do you even have this, if you don't mind me asking. Don't get me wrong, I'm incredibly grateful it's here."

"I got some money a few years back. Once I paid off everything that needed paying off and bulked up my savings, I still had a nice chunk left over. So I thought, hey I have space in my garage and sledges are cool."

Claire nodded slowly, still examining the controls. "Okay. But it's not like Squire's Isle gets days like this very often."

"Three, since I got it. We've had three days where the whole town's been snowed in, and no one could get out. Older people need medicine, kid needs diapers, someone needs something, and I'm there. It's nice to be useful."

"Yeah." Claire smiled. "I get that."

"You know how to run one of these things, right?" he asked next to her ear.

"Jodie taught me to ride a motorcycle a while back." She patted the right handlebar. "Gas on the right, release to slow down." She patted the left handlebar. "Brake."

Hoagie said, "Sounds good to me. Take it nice and easy."

Claire started the engine and gave it some gas. The snowmobile lunged, but she managed to get it under control before she and its owner were bucked into the snow.

"If you wreck my sledge, who do I call to arrest you?"

Behind her mask, Claire smiled.

Chapter Twelve

She dropped Hoagie at his house, then headed out to Spence Alley. She was grateful he'd been there for the first leg, just to confirm she really knew how to run the snowmobile. He insisted on calling it a sledge, and she decided she might as well call it that, too. She parked the sledge in front of Guy's house. By the time she dismounted, he was out on the porch watching her.

"You bringing me more trouble?"

"I could take it elsewhere," she said.

He shrugged. "Routine is routine, but it gets pretty boring. We like the excitement." He gestured vaguely at the other houses. "I talked to the neighbors this morning, and they all agree it's worth a little trouble to get rid of these putzes. Whatever you need, we'll be happy to provide."

"I appreciate it, Mister..."

"Told ya last night. Just Guy is fine."

She nodded. "Okay. I'll be going back over there this morning. Will you keep an eye on the sledge?"

"Um-hmm," he said, which seemed to be an affirmative. "Need my rifle?"

She considered it, but shook her head. "I think I want to keep my hands free. But I'm armed. Hopefully it'll be enough."

"Good luck."

Claire made sure she had her kit, saluted Guy, and marched into the woods.

The trees provided shelter from the wind, and the canopy overhead had prevented the snow from getting too deep on the path she had to take.

It was obviously much easier traversing the space between the two roads in daylight, and she arrived in a fraction of the time it had taken her the night before. She crouched and then stretched out on her stomach, using a slight rise in the ground for cover as she examined the clustered houses ahead of her.

The big house was to her right, with two houses on either side of the road in front of it. She took out her kit, unzipped it, and retrieved her binoculars. The snow around the houses was a crisp and unbroken field of marshmallow fluff. It reminded her of looking out at clouds from an airplane window, shimmering in the morning sun. The only sign of life was a dotted line of footsteps leading from the main house to the house where the women were being held. It looked as if someone had made the journey at least a few times.

The generators still hummed loudly enough to cover any minor noises she made, but footprints would be a problem. She couldn't skulk around as easily as she had the night before. She calculated a route she could take to the back door without her passage being spotted from the main house and kept it in mind as she observed the tableau in front of her.

Lights in the main house, smoke rising from the chimney, generator chugging in its back yard. Only one other house besides where the women were being held had the same signs of being occupied. She assumed the other two houses had been claimed by Lile and Packard, or they were all doubled-up. Either way, she didn't intend to waste much time on the two houses closest to the main road.

The footprints implied the women had been fed that morning. She didn't see Wyman as the type of captor who made regular welfare checks on his inmates, so she felt confident she had a little time. She got to her feet and moved quickly. She stayed low and made long strides, hoping that if her tracks *were* spotted, they might be mistaken for some kind of wild animal on the hunt.

She reached the back of the women's house and pressed her back against the wall. She knocked softly on the door and waited. She unholstered her gun and kept it low by her side on the off chance one of the men was inside and came to investigate. Nothing from inside, so she knocked again. On the third knock, there was a knock in return.

"Tereza?" she said, her voice just loud enough to be heard on the other side.

"Sheriff Claire?"

"That's right. Are you alone in there?"

"I am with the women."

Claire said, "But just them? None of the men are with you?"

"No, not right now. They came to give us food. Nothing else for a few hours more."

That was fantastic news. "Okay. I'm going to try to come in. Hold tight."

She holstered her gun and took her kit out. Lockpicking had never really been one of her strongest skills, but the door didn't exactly seem like Fort Knox. She suspected Wyman had used terror to keep the women contained as much as anything else. They were in a strange country, probably had no idea exactly where they were, and nowhere to run even if they did get out of the house. There was just no reason for him to waste much effort on the locks.

She hoped.

Claire bent her knees to get eye-level with the lock. She had to take off her gloves to manipulate the tools, and the cold was already numbing her fingers. She didn't let it distract her. In a matter of seconds she heard the lock click and tried the knob. It twisted freely, but the door had warped in its frame. She had to give it a few solid tugs before it came free, and she almost tumbled backward into the snow. Hoping the noise wasn't loud enough to attract attention, she stepped into the house and pulled the door shut behind her.

A woman was standing close enough to the door that she had to step back when Claire came inside. She was tall and extremely skinny, but in a way that seemed more genetic than starvation. Her black hair was center-parted around a striking pale face, and her eyes were wide with shock, surprise, and fear as she accepted there really might be a savior standing in front of her.

"Tereza?" Claire asked.

The woman nodded. They were standing in a kitchen equipped with the barest essentials: table, chairs, sink, icebox in the corner. The overhead lights were off, but the sun reflecting off the snow shined in through the window to make the room plenty bright. Another woman was standing behind Tereza, with two more hiding in the hallway. Only their heads were visible as they peeked around opposite sides of the doorway.

"You said there were five of you...?"

"Mila is in the house," the woman behind Tereza said. Her voice was thickly accented by a Slavic first language Claire couldn't pinpoint. "I am Vera. They are Stefaniya and Kseniya."

Claire nodded to them. She didn't recognize any of the women, so she assumed Mila was the one she'd seen in the window.

"My name is Claire. I'm the sheriff of Squire's... of the place where you are right now. I was hoping you'd all be together so I could get you all out at once."

"Out?" Stefaniya said.

"Somewhere safe," Claire said.

"They'll follow us."

"I'm working on that. But the important thing is getting you away from them."

She brushed her hand over her mouth as she thought through her options. She looked down and noticed another potential flaw in her plan: all the women were barefoot.

"Where are your shoes?"

Vera answered. "Why would we need shoes? They don't expect us to go anywhere."

The snow between them and Guy's house might be relatively shallow, but there was no way she'd ask them to make the journey without shoes.

"Damn," she muttered. "That throws a wrench in things."

"I told you," Vera growled at Tereza. "You were a fool to hope."

Claire said, "I'm still going to do everything in my power to get you out. All of you. It's just complicated."

"Sure you will."

Claire stepped around Tereza and met Vera's gaze. "These assholes killed a friend of mine. They tried to hurt my wife and they set fire to my squad car. I'm getting you out because it's the right thing to do, but also because they've spent the past few days pissing me the hell off, and I'm not going to let them get away with that. If you won't believe I'm doing it for altruistic reasons, then believe I'm doing it because I want to win."

Vera didn't blink. She tightened her jaw, glanced at the women in the hallway, and seemed to relax just a hair.

"They give us exactly what we need and no more," she said. "That means socks, but no shoes. Food, but we can't cook it or use silverware. Only plastic utensils."

"How often do they check on you?"

"Every few hours," Tereza said. "Daylight, midday, dinner time. Sometimes they come over to check on us at random times or to get someone else to help in the house."

Vera said, "They probably won't come over much with all the snow. They don't very much like to be uncomfortable."

"I supposed that's good for me," Claire said. "If I have to leave you here when I go, I want to at least get some information. You can start by telling me where you came from."

Unsurprisingly, it was Vera who spoke. "I will tell you my story, and then you will have heard all of our stories." She crossed her arms over her chest. "I am from Solnechny. A student. I have two jobs, no money. A woman approached, said she needs workers. Great pay. Double what I'm making from both jobs combined." She wrinkled her nose and looked away. "I was stupid."

"Desperate," Tereza said.

"I'm sure you all were," Claire said. "Desperation has a way of making smart people overlook warning signs that seem obvious in retrospect."

Vera sighed. "Well, I agreed. She drove me out of town... long, long way to the coast. It was dark by the time we arrived, and men came up to the car. Opened the door, shined lights in my face. They took my wallet, my phone. Told me to get out and walk with them or they'd beat me. I did what I was told. I had no idea where I was or how I could get home, so..."

"We were put on a boat," Tereza said. "Put down below in a... a... metal casket. We were there for days. Barely any food. Only enough water to keep us from collapsing. Eventually they took us up onto the deck. At night, of course. After this, we only ever saw night. They put us in a little boat and it took us between into a... a..."

"An inlet," Kseniya muttered.

"Mm." Tereza swallowed a lump in her throat. "We arrived here, and that is when these men took us. They never spoke to us. They spoke to each other about us. Like they were buying furniture."

Claire pushed down her anger. "How many of you were there to begin with?"

"Ten, at first," Vera said. "The others went, one at a time. We never knew when one would leave for good. They always went to the house first, so the men can be certain she is capable of certain duties."

"Did they rape you?"

Vera smiled darkly. "Oh no. Never. Some men will pay extra for a virgin, so they don't dare risk it. And they take our word for it. Something to be grateful for."

Claire's skin crawled. "How much time generally passes between someone going to the main house and leaving for good?"

"It depends," Tereza said.

Claire said, "This weather would probably throw it off anyway. The ferries have been shut down, so they couldn't get to a buyer even if he has one lined up."

Stefaniya's brow wrinkled. "Fairies?"

"Yeah... oh. Uh, ferry." She spelled it. "Big boats that take people to the mainland."

Tereza said, "Mainland? Where are we?"

"An island. Squire's Isle."

"He was right," Vera said. "There really is nowhere for us to run. We're stuck here."

Claire said, "That is absolutely wrong. We'll get you away from here, and then we'll figure things out from there. We'll get in touch with the embassy, inform them about what's happened. We're going to get you home."

Vera looked unconvinced, but Claire could see the beginning of hope in Tereza's face. She had a feeling the other two would go along with what their leaders decided.

She stepped closer to the kitchen door so she could get a clearer picture of the house. There was a hallway with a bathroom and an empty laundry room between the kitchen and the living room. Two open doors on the far wall were open to reveal bedrooms barely large enough for the two mattresses crammed into each one. Tereza seemed to know what she was thinking.

"Sometimes we alternate and take the couch. Sometimes we all squeeze together in one room, if it's a cold night."

Claire nodded. Not a whole lot of hiding places if Wyman or one of his people came over. The windows of the living room were covered with plywood, a precautionary move against high winds, but they were loose enough that someone could see out. She turned to face the women again.

"Kseniya, go watch out the window and tell me if any of them starts over here." The woman, who couldn't be much older than twenty, hurried to do what she was told. Claire waited until she was in position and then addressed the other three.

"Wyman can't take Mila anywhere until the weather clears. He's as trapped on this island as you are. I intend to take advantage of that. I know it seems hopeless, but I specialize in hopeless. You have a sheriff standing here, promising you that she's going to fight to get you to safety. Forty-eight hours ago, that probably seemed impossible, too."

Tereza and Vera exchanged a look, said nothing. Claire sighed.

"I told Tereza my name was Claire Curran, but that's my married name. I have another name. It's more famous. I'm Claire Lance."

They stared blankly at her.

"Lance," she repeated. "Bank robbery... falsely accused of..." She looked at Kseniya, who also looked completely lost. Claire sang, "I'm through with games and I'm ending this dance...?" No reaction. "I guess it takes a while for songs to get to Solnechny, huh?"

"If you need to find me," Stefaniya sang so quietly she almost couldn't be heard, "I'm on the road with Lance." She lifted her head and finally met Claire's eye. "That is you? You're... her?"

"That's right."

Stefaniya looked at Vera. "I trust her."

"What is Lance?" Tereza said.

Claire took a deep breath. "It's a long story."

Vera said, "We have time, Claire Lance."

Claire looked at Kseniya, who was still watching out the window.

"It started about twelve years ago, when I was a detective in Chicago..."

***

The women listened intently to her story. Vera remained standing in front of Claire for the duration. Tereza retreated to the couch and sat on the sinking cushions, her head hanging low by the time Claire got to the part about Montana. When she finished the whole story, even Vera looked impressed.

"I did all of that knowing I risked everything if I was found out. I could have been taken to prison. It was extremely close a couple of times, actually. But I kept going because I couldn't just stand by and let it happen. I put my freedom and my life on the line time and time again. The only difference this time is I don't have to worry about anyone finding out who I really am. I was fighting with one hand tied behind my back."

Vera looked at Tereza, who showed her palms and shrugged. She looked back at Claire. "No."

"I'm sorry?"

"The risk is too much. We can't let you do that."

Claire laughed incredulously. "You can't be serious. I'm not going to let these guys continue doing this on my island. Freeing you is part of the deal. If you're worried about my safety, don't."

"These men hurt so many people already..."

"They're still hurting people, Vera. You. Tereza. All of you." She looked around the room. "I didn't come here to ask permission to save you."

"But if you ask us to go and we refuse..."

"I'll take your asses into custody until we figure out what to do with you. This is not a negotiation."

"What do you need from us?"

"Schedules. You must have some idea when the men are asleep, when they go into town for supplies. Everyone has their routines, and I doubt this group is any different. We can use that to our advantage."

Vera said, "We're not sure about days. But I believe two of them go for groceries every Saturday or Sunday. It's very easy to lose track of time here."

"Of course," Claire said. "Do they sleep in shifts?"

"One of them is always awake," Tereza said. "Lights are on all the time, at least. Sometimes one of them comes over here in the middle of the night to make sure we are all tucked up tight."

Claire grimaced. "Well, that's awful. We can work with that, though. If they only come here a few times a day—"

Kseniya suddenly moved away from the window. "One of the men is coming!"

Claire immediately left the living room and went into the laundry room. Gaping holes for water hookups and ventilation had been sloppily plugged to keep the weather out. Vera had followed Claire.

"Just act the way you always do when one of them comes by." Vera nodded and reached for the doorknob to pull it shut, but Claire stopped her. "No, a closed door is suspicious. Just don't draw any attention to the hallway. Go!"

She stepped behind the door and held the knob to pin herself between it and the wall. She could see the living room through the crack by the hinges. Vera looked into the crack, looked at the door, and then hurried out of sight. Less than a minute later, the front door opened and brought with it a rush of freezing air. Every door and window in the house rattled with the sudden gust, and trembled again as the new arrival slammed the door behind himself.

"Whoo, it's damn cold out there! How you ladies holding up?"

Claire had no way to be certain, but she guessed this was Jesse, the only man who hadn't been part of the conversation she overheard. None of the women answered him, but he moved through the living room without pausing, so it seemed he hadn't been expecting a response. He passed by Claire's hiding place, confirming his identity, and went into the kitchen.

"Hey-hey, V," he said. "Mr. W said on account of the weather we could give you ladies some hot chocolate to drink. Isn't that nice of him?" More silence. This time Jesse didn't seem as willing to let it go. "Ladies, I don't want to go back and tell him you were rude or ungrateful..."

"Thank you," Vera said.

The others also said it at various volumes, but it seemed to be enough. "Good girls. Now go on and get the cups down, I'll pour everyone a mug. Kissy, Stefanie, get in here, too."

She heard the sound of cups being put on the table, and pouring. Kseniya glanced at the laundry room as she passed, but hopefully too quickly for Jesse to notice.

"How much..." Tereza said, but the words seemed to get caught in her throat. "I mean, h-how long do... do you think..."

Vera said, "When is the weather supposed to clear?"

"Hell if I know," Jesse said. "Mr. W thinks it'll be clear enough to drive in a few days. Don't you worry, though, we'll keep taking real good care of you. Your friend in the house is gonna make you some stew tonight. Doesn't that sound tasty, ladies?"

"Yes," someone said so quietly that Claire couldn't tell which it was.

"I better get back. Anything specific you ladies need next time someone comes over to say hi?"

There was a silence. Then Stefaniya said, "There's something..."

Claire tensed. She moved her free hand to her holster.

"Yeah? Spit it out, sweetheart."

"There's..."

If any of the other women stepped in, Jesse might suspect they were keeping a secret. She envisioned a scenario where she had to take out Jesse and secure him somewhere. Wyman wasn't likely to ignore one of his men vanishing into thin air.

"Feminine things," Stefaniya finally said.

Jesse grunted. "God, shit, ladies. I don't know. Just... I don't know, make due with whatever you have here, or something. We don't have anything like that."

He left the kitchen in a hurry, passing the laundry room without a glance back. The door opened, inviting in another blast of arctic air, and then slammed shut. Claire stayed where she was as Tereza hurried past with a whispered, "Wait, wait." She stood still for a full minute until Tereza said, "Okay, he's back inside the main house."

Claire stepped out to see Vera glaring at Stefaniya, who had been backed up against a counter as if anticipating a blow. "Ladies? Everything okay?"

"She was going to tell him about you," Vera snapped. "She was a coward and could have gotten us all killed."

"She wasn't a coward," Claire said. "It just took her a little longer to find her strength. She's scared. I know you're all terrified. These people have given you shelter, food. I'm offering you a very dangerous idea. I'd be surprised if none of you had considered telling him about me. In fact, I suspect one reason you're so angry, Vera, is because you were thinking about doing the same thing."

Vera looked away. "She could have gotten you killed," she said again.

"Yeah, but she didn't." She nodded to Stefaniya. "Thank you."

Tereza remained by the window to watch for more visitors. "But what do we do now? We can't leave. You can't stay here and hide in the room whenever someone comes in.'

Vera said, "She will leave. She is leaving, right?"

"But I'm coming back."

"Sure, sure, yes." Vera chuckled softly. "Go on. Back to your town."

Claire considered her next move very carefully. It was stupid, reckless, and actually illegal. But she unclipped her holster and pulled out her gun. She gripped it by the barrel and held it out to Vera.

"What are you doing?"

"Giving back a little bit of power these assholes have taken away from you. Forcing you to say please and thank you for the bare necessities. Hell, not even providing the bare necessities. That's how they break you. It's how they make you dependent on them, keep you too scared to run when the opportunity presents itself."

Vera stared at the gun, then looked into Claire's eyes.

"Keep it."

"Are you sure?"

"Yes. You will be our gun, Claire Lance."

Claire put the gun back in her holster. "I have to leave, but I'm not going to be gone. Not by a long shot. Would anyone be able to tell if that back door was left open?"

Tereza said, "I don't know. Maybe. But we can unlock it for you if you come back."

"When I come back," Claire corrected. "I'm not abandoning you. This wasn't a wasted trip. I know what you need, what to bring you when I come back. And more importantly, you know I'm out there working to get you free. I'm going to do everything in my power to help you."

"Thank you," Vera said.

Claire went to the back door and glanced down. A boot print was smeared in mud and snow on the threshold of the house. She stared at it, frozen at the implications.

"Is there any chance he saw that?" she asked.

Vera came closer and stiffened. "No... no, he couldn't have."

"You're positive?"

She thought, then nodded. "Yes, I'm sure. He came in and went directly to the table. He poured the drink and then left quickly. The door was not in his line of sight."

"Do you have a towel?" Kseniya retrieved one and Claire crouched down to wipe away the incriminating mark. She looked for more but didn't see anything. She hadn't ventured far into the house, and there wasn't all that much space to cover, but she still wanted to be thorough. She handed the towel back and stood up. "Look carefully. Make sure I didn't just screw this all up."

Kseniya nodded and went into the laundry room to check the floor.

Vera said, "We will be fine until you come back. We are familiar with the way things are. The only thing you've changed is adding hope. That will only be cruel if you don't succeed."

Claire held out her hand. "Then I better do everything in my power to win."

Vera took Claire's hand, squeezed. "Thank you, Claire Lance."

"Curran. I kind of like it better these days."

"I understand," Vera said.

Claire looked past her to Tereza. "Are we still clear?"

Tereza said, "No one in or out."

"Okay. I'll be back as soon as I can."

Vera said, "Good luck."

Claire opened the back door, stepped out into the cold, and pulled the door shut behind her. She stayed completely still, listening for movement from the main house, but all she heard was the hum of generators. She realized she could spend the whole day hunkered there against the wall in fear of someone glancing out the window at the exact wrong second, so she pushed away and retraced her steps in the snow. She ducked around a tree and leaned a shoulder against the bark. No shout of surprise, no crunch of running steps in pursuit, no gunfire.

She exhaled a plume of thick white haze and continued her escape, running back through the woods to Guy's house and the sledge.

CHAPTER THIRTEEN

CLAIRE NEEDED shoes, coats, guns, and a vehicle large enough to carry five women from Wyman's little compound to town. Everything but the guns were necessities, and she hoped the guns would prove to just be a deterrent to Wyman and his morons trying anything stupid. Rescue was definitely doable, but she had to get started immediately. She expected Wyman would want to make up for lost time as soon as the ferry was back on schedule.

Hoagie had told her to keep the sledge for as long as she needed, so she returned directly to the mayor's residence and parked at the front door. Jodie hurried out before Claire was even fully dismounted, pulling her into a desperate hug.

"You okay?" Jodie whispered against the side of Claire's head.

"I'm fine. I'm okay."

Jodie held her for a few breaths longer, then stepped back and squeezed her shoulders. "I heard the engine from about half a mile away. Patricia and Jill are making you hot chocolate."

"That sounds amazing." She looped her arm around Jill's and led her back inside. "Was everything quiet here while I was gone?"

"Completely," Jodie said. "Patricia spent most of the time in her office, but Jill and I were in charge of entertaining a little girl with more energy than seventeen puppies. I took her out in the garage and showed her how a car's engine works, so I think I'm like Wonder Woman to her."

Claire smiled and kissed Jodie's temple. "Good job, Joe."

They stopped in the foyer where Jodie helped Claire escape from her layers. "What about you? The actual dangerous thing."

It already felt more like a dream than anything she'd actually done. Those abandoned homes and their dark corners, bare-bones furnishings, and humming generators was a whole different world from the mayor's residence. She explained what happened as best she could, starting over when Jill and Patricia came out to join them. Patricia was visibly angry by the time Claire finished.

"I can't believe that's happening on my island right now. Those women are being held prisoner here *right now* and I can't do anything."

"We are doing something," Claire said. "We have to worry about their safety. If we move too fast or get reckless, Wyman could do something drastic. Going slow may feel like wasting time, but it's the right move in this case."

Patricia sighed and crossed her arms over her chest. "I'll trust you. But if this isn't wrapped up by the time the ferry service starts up again..."

Claire didn't let her finish the thought. "If that happens, I'll make the call myself. I swear."

Patricia nodded.

"Right now, I need shoes and coats. The rest of the plan won't matter if those women can't set foot out of their prison."

Jill took out her phone and poised her thumbs to type. "What are their names? The women?"

"Tereza. Vera. Stefaniya. Mila. Kseniya. I'm not sure of the spelling on any of those."

"That's fine." Jill poked the screen and the phone in Patricia's hand pinged. Claire knew she had just received the list. "I didn't like just thinking of them as 'the women.'"

Claire nodded. "I'll tell you a little about their personalities later, when we have some time."

"Thank you."

Patricia said, "Pass." Jill looked at her, confused, and Patricia shook her head and looked down at her feet. "It's hard enough knowing they're up there. If I get to know them, I'll just keep getting angrier and angrier..."

Jill put a hand on her arm. "Okay, hon. Okay."

"After," Patricia said to Claire. "I'll get to know them when this is all over."

"Right."

"I can make some calls," Jill said. "Some of the other teachers may know where we can get hold of some shoes and coats."

Claire said, "The tricky part will be the vehicle. The plows haven't started on the country roads yet, so an ordinary car or truck won't cut it and we can't afford to wait. Mayor... Patricia... you really came through with Hoagie. I don't suppose you know anyone on the island who has a tank?"

Patricia shook her head and then tilted her head to the side. "Not a tank... but I think something that may work just as well. How exposed is the clearing where these houses are?"

Claire shrugged. "There's definitely tree-cover, but it's generally open skies."

"Is there enough room for a helicopter to land?"

Claire's eyebrows shot up. "You can get your hands on a helicopter?"

Jill's smile lit up her whole face. "Our son works at the airport."

***

The last time Claire visited the island's small airport, she'd been a fugitive arranging what she hoped to be a one-way flight to Alaska. She hadn't had occasion to visit the actual terminal, a small building attached to twin hangars that ran the length of the runway. She spent over an hour at the Hood-Colby dining room table working out the plan with her co-conspirators, two of which kept getting called away to deal with the child in the house. By the time Claire put her thick winter gear back on, she felt she had a solid plan to put into action.

If she could get her hands on a helicopter, that is.

She left Jodie and the Hood-Colbys to gather shoes and coats and headed out on the sledge. The main roads had mostly been cleared by plows enough for emergency travel, but no one on the island seemed to be taking advantage of it besides her. Duckworth Airport was the same as she remembered it, save for the fact the stand of trees flanking it on three sides were now dusted in snow and perfectly postcard-ready. A four-by-four jacked up high on its chassis stood in front of the airport's main entrance. Claire parked behind the truck and headed inside.

The terminal was a large room that reminded Claire of a high school hallway, all polished tile and gleaming walls. A sign to the right advertised flights to the mainland with a list of prices, and to her left was a small luncheonette which was currently dark. Straight ahead was a curving counter with a large model of a helicopter on display behind it.

"Hello?" she called.

A young man came out of an office behind the helicopter counter. He was in his early twenties, with close-cropped black hair and an impressively thick beard. He wore a plaid shirt under a puffy black coat. He smiled when he saw her.

"Sheriff. I'm Michael Colby."

"No Hood-hyphen?" she asked as she accepted his outstretched hand.

"Long story. Patricia is my birth mom, but Jill is more than my stepmom, so... it's for her." He shrugged. "I never really liked the hyphen thing anyway. More streamlined."

Claire said, "Okay."

"They said you needed a helicopter."

"And they told me you had one."

"Well, I have access to one." He hooked a thumb over his shoulder. "Tours are Paige's company, but she didn't want to risk getting out in this weather. She's willing to let me take you wherever you need to go. Mom didn't tell me much about why you needed it, but I assume it's something important. Someone missing?"

Claire shook her head. "Do you have a map of the island?"

"Sure." He pointed at the flights counter and led her over. He went behind the desk and crouched down to retrieve something from a cabinet underneath.

Claire said, "So if you're not the helicopter guy, what do you do?"

"Pilot," he said. "Just hopping from here to the mainland and back again, but flying is flying."

He stood up and unrolled a map on top of the counter. Claire tilted her head to get her bearings. When she found the spot where Wyman and his people were, she traced a line back to Spence Alley.

"Could you land the chopper there?"

He looked closely. "Does the canopy still look like that?"

"Honestly, I don't remember. It might be a little more open. I remember a lot of moonlight coming down, and it didn't seem to stop the snow from accumulating."

Michael pulled a face and scratched a thumb over his beard. "Hm. It's not ideal. How deep is the snow?"

"Ankle?"

"That's not too bad. But if it's fresh, landing might cause a mini-blizzard. Whiteout. But it's manageable for a good pilot."

"Are you a good pilot?"

Michael hesitated before he answered, which she appreciated. Finally, he nodded. "I can do it. I wouldn't even try for just anyone, but for the sheriff... absolutely. Yes."

"How many passengers? We're going after five people."

"Room for seven passengers," he said. "Five shouldn't be a problem unless there's a weight issue."

She shook her head. "They're all very petite. When can the helicopter be ready to head out?"

"I just need to make sure it's fueled up, run a quick check to make sure nothing's iced up. I should be ready whenever you give the go-ahead."

They exchanged numbers and Claire told him to be ready to go at a moment's notice. He promised he would, and he'd text her updates if he ran into any hiccups.

On her way out of the airport, she took out her phone and dialed Randall's number. Until now, she'd been happy to leave him in charge of their prisoners. But now she needed another cop for the rescue mission, and she trusted him more than any of their volunteers. He picked up as she reached the glass doors of the terminal and she stopped so she wouldn't have to raise her voice over the wind.

"Everything under control with our guests?"

"The one we have here is complaining about how cold the cells are. Poor baby. The one in the hospital seems to be in too much pain to put up much of a front. If you ever have an argument with your wife, I want you to know I'm taking her side."

Claire smiled. "That's probably smart, Randall. How many volunteers do you have with you at the station right now?"

"Three. Harvey Moses, Chip, and Ami."

Good people, all of them. That was a relief. "I need you to leave one of them in charge. Harvey Moses is my choice, but I'll leave it up to you."

"Where am I going?"

"The mayor's residence," Claire said. "I'm going to need backup."

***

The sky was already beginning to darken when Claire left the airport. The day felt endless but it also felt far too early for the sun to go down. It didn't matter. She wasn't going to let those women spend one more night in that house. It was actually ideal if she arrived at night; darkness would help conceal their escape. She went over the plan in her mind on the drive back to the mayor's residence.

"The generators might cover the noise of the snowmobile," Jodie had said, "but there's no way they'd miss a helicopter landing next door."

"That's why we're not arriving in the helicopter," Claire said. "It's our getaway driver. I go in on the sledge with shoes and coats. I get the women out and through the woods to safety. Guy's house. Once we're in place, we call in the chopper. It lands, the women get aboard, and it takes them to a secure location."

Patricia said, "Leaving Guy and his neighbors to deal with some very pissed off criminals."

"I'm not going alone," Claire said. "Deputy White will come up with me, and I'm going to leave him on the ground while I go with the ladies."

"You're going to leave him behind?" Jodie said.

Claire shrugged. "It's hardly ideal, I know. Everything in me wants to be the person who stays behind and fights the bad guy. But these women have been through a terrible ordeal, and I wouldn't feel right sending them off with any type of male authority figure. Besides, Wyman seems like the type of guy who would come at me hard just because I'm a woman. I have a feeling he'll be more likely to surrender if he's facing off against Randall."

Jodie lifted her hand. "I want to be clear that I wasn't complaining about the plan where you get in a helicopter and fly away from danger."

Claire smirked and took her hand, kissed the fingers, and kept hold of it.

The part of the plan she was most concerned about was the fifth woman, the one staying in the main house. There wouldn't be a way to sneak her out, so she would have to be last. That was where the plan had the biggest chance of falling apart. But she wasn't going to leave anyone behind to serve as a hostage or, worst case scenario, a lesson in what happens when someone makes Dennis Wyman angry.

She arrived at the mayor's residence at the same time Randall pulled around the corner in the town's only remaining squad car. Another car was parked in front of the house's main entrance. Claire parked and dismounted as he rolled to a stop behind her.

"Damn, Claire. You get a promotion and you start riding in style."

"Trust me, I'd take the cruiser any day. You'll get to ride it soon enough."

A tall black woman was with Jill in the living room. They were bent over a box, and Jill straightened up to wave Claire in.

"Sheriff Curran, this is Sonia Edwards. Sonia, this is Claire."

Sonia offered her hand in such a way that Claire had to resist the urge to curtsey. "Considering your profession," Sonia said as Claire shook her hand, "I hope it isn't rude to say I'm glad we've never met before this."

"Not at all. But it's nice to meet you now." Claire looked at the box. "Is this..."

Sonia said, "Clothing drive loot! Jill said you needed shoes and coats, but she wasn't terribly specific, but I grabbed what we had at the school." She reached into the bag and pulled out a coat at random. "The coats aren't really gender specific. I'm sure it'll be okay if they're a little bulky. Shoes are trickier."

Claire dug through the box and tried to picture what she'd seen at the house. "I didn't really pay much attention to their feet other than noticing they didn't have shoes. None of them seemed to be particularly freakish one way or the other."

"We can err on the side of caution," Sonia said. "Bigger shoes with the laces tied tight are always better than trying to cram your toes into something too small."

"Right," Claire said.

Patricia came into the room with a large backpack. "Claire, welcome back. Hello, Deputy. I was trying to find something for you to carry all this stuff up there." She held the bag open. "We used this last time we went camping. I'm positive you can fit a few shoes and coats in there."

"That's great, Patricia," Claire said. "Thank you. You've both been amazing. I have no idea what I would have done without the two of you running point on this. I wouldn't even have been able to get up there to see what's happening if you hadn't gotten Hoagie's sledge for me."

Patricia said, "Just don't ask for a snowmobile the next time the department's budget comes up."

"I'll try not to push my luck," Claire said. "We're already going to need a new squad car." She looked around the room. "Where's Jodie?"

"Kitchen."

Claire excused herself and went through the house. Jodie was at the stove, checking something on her phone before she picked up the wooden spoon.

"I thought when we got married, we agreed cooking was going to be my wifely duty."

"We did."

Claire wrapped her arms around Jodie from behind. "Does this mean I have to start taking out the trash?"

Jodie put down the spoon, resting her hands on top of Claire's arms. "It means I feel pretty useless with all this going on. I can't get you clothes and I don't know anyone who happens to have a damn helicopter in their garage, but I can make sure you're fueled up and full of energy before you go riding to the rescue."

"It smells amazing." She pressed her face into Jodie's hair. "Mm. So do you."

"Careful. That's the mayor's shampoo you're admiring."

"Mm, no, I recognize that. And I know what you smell like." She nibbled on Jodie's earlobe. "Thank you for thinking of this, Joe. You know I wouldn't have bothered otherwise."

"That's what I'm here for. I take care of you when you're too tunnel vision to do it yourself." She turned around in Claire's arms. "I'm terrified, you know."

"Of this? This is a couple of douchebags with guns. This is nothing."

Jodie said, "You told me Wyman was smart. He's crafty. He might outthink you or..."

"We'll worry about that when and if it happens. Right now we only have to be focused on getting those women out of danger."

"Yeah." She stepped back and smoothed her hands over the shoulders of Claire's uniform shirt. "Wow, you're a mess."

"It's been a long day."

Jodie toyed with Claire's collar. "Do you remember the day you told me your real name?"

Claire nodded. "I was falling in love with you. And I didn't want that to happen while I was lying to you. But I knew telling you the truth might make you run like hell. Telling you was the scariest thing I've ever done." She cupped Jodie's cheek. "Worked out pretty good, though."

"Yeah." Jodie smiled. "Did I ever tell you what made me come back after I left?"

"You forgot your shoes."

Jodie smiled. "Right. I got all the way to the lobby and realized I was in my socks. I realized it was night time, and there were muggers and rapists and other various assholes out there in the dark. I stood there and thought about what a dangerous world it was. How scary it was. And I realized I didn't feel any of that scariness when I was with you. You said you were innocent, but I had no reason to believe what you said. Of course a fugitive would claim she didn't really do it, and you'd just admitted that you'd lied to me since the day we met."

Claire nodded but stayed silent.

"I realized that the woman I'd been spending time with couldn't be a murderer. Or if you had murdered someone, it would be in a way that made sense to me. You know? Self-defense, or they were assholes. I figured I knew you well enough to make that assessment, and that was all that mattered."

"When you came back up, you said you'd forgotten my real name."

Jodie smiled. "I had. You were still Carmen to me, despite what happened. That said a lot."

"Not that I mind the trip down memory lane," Claire said, "but I assume you're going somewhere with this."

Jodie touched the badge on Claire's chest. "You don't change, Claire. You get older, smarter, more cautious. Your clothes change. Your name changes. But the woman standing in front of me right now is the woman I married, who is the woman that spent so many years running from the law, who helped rob a bank to expose very bad people. You're the same woman who loved Elaine and was a Chicago cop. You were probably the same person as a kid, just shorter.

"You're there when people need you. Those women need you now. So I'm not going to ask you to stay here and wait for the feds. I'm going to give you the tools you need to go up there and be you."

"I love you, Jodie."

"I love you, too. That was a really good speech."

"Thanks." She pecked Claire's lips, then turned it into a more involved kiss. She stepped back and looked into Claire's eyes. "Always go. Always do what you have to. But always do whatever you can to come home to me, okay?"

Claire said, "I swear."

Jodie nodded. She put a hand over Claire's badge. "Your armor." She moved the hand to the holster on Claire's hip. "Your sword."

Claire put her hand over Jodie's heart. "My real armor."

"Sally forth, brave knight," Jodie said. "Let me finish your dinner."

Claire kissed Jodie once more and backed away, reluctantly leaving her. She stopped at the door and looked back. Jodie was at the stove, stirring the pot as steam rose in thin wisps around her.

Her wife.

She smiled and went back to the other room to finish going through the donated clothes.

***

After dinner, Isabel demanded her new best friend Jodie put her to bed with a story. Patricia and Jill both attempted to intervene, but Jodie was thrilled to do it. The alternative would be staying downstairs while Claire and Randall finished packing up their supplies and headed out. She knew she couldn't be there for that. So she and Claire had a quiet, private goodbye in the dark kitchen and then she headed upstairs with her favorite seven-year-old.

The nursery was a beautiful room at the very top of the stairs, with orange and blue walls. Toys were scattered over the floor in a sort of organized chaos, and the shelves were stuffed full with books. Isabel, already bathed, brushed, and put in pajamas by Patricia, ran to her bed and hopped up onto the cushion of blankets. She pressed back against the pillows and began burrowing into the blankets.

"What book do you want to read?" Jodie asked.

"You tell me one!" Isabel said.

Jodie sat on the edge of the bed, twisting to face the girl. "Oh. I'm not really good with stories. I know, um... Snow White. I could probably tell you most of *The Princess Bride*..."

"No, a *new* one," Isabel demanded. "Tell me a story you make up."

Jodie laughed. "You don't ask for much, do you?"

She pinched Isabel's foot through the blanket. Downstairs she heard something heavy hit the floor. She looked toward the door and then back to the innocent little girl waiting to be told a story.

"Okay. I have a story. Once upon a time, there was a queen without a kingdom. She was thrown out of her home, and a bunch of really bad people chased her to punish her for something she hadn't done. She ran, ran, ran, as far as she could, but the people still hunted her down wherever she went. And in one of those places, she met a queen of her own. Someone who loved her and wanted her to be safe and protected no matter what. After that, they ran together.

"Then, one day, the people of her kingdom forgave the queen. She was free. But she didn't want to go back to where she'd been so very sad. She didn't want to keep running into those people who thought she was a bad queen, and she wanted a fresh start." She smiled. "Also her new wife, the co-queen, didn't like the old kingdom very much and didn't want to live there, so they compromised."

Isabel squirmed and tried to keep her eyes open. "Did they live happily ev'rafter?"

Jodie heard voices downstairs. "For a long time, they did. They had a very nice life in their new home. But then some very bad people wanted to take away the queen's kingdom. They told her she needed to just sit down and be quiet and let them do whatever they wanted. She said absolutely not."

"I like her." Isabel's voice was slurred on the edge of sleep.

Jodie smiled. "I do, too. These bad people hurt one of the queen's friends very badly. They tried to hurt the queen's new wife. So the queen decided it was time to kick them out of the kingdom."

"Good..."

She looked at Isabel, whose eyes were barely open. She stroked the girl's hair away from her face and tucked the blanket tighter around her shoulders. She bent down and pressed a kiss to Isabel's forehead.

"Good night, Izzy."

Jodie got up and turned off the overhead light. Jill had mentioned the bird lamp next to the closet was a nightlight. She went to it, switched it on, and that corner of the room was awash in soft golden-orange glow. She heard the front door close downstairs and pushed back the sense of dread that clawed at her spine. She looked at the bed, where Isabel seemed to already be asleep, so she moved on the balls of her feet to the window. She pushed aside the curtain and looked down at the front lawn of the house.

She heard the snowmobile's engine, then saw it pull away from the house and slip across the slush that had accumulated on the driveway. Claire was driving with Randall behind her, the bulky backpack strapped to his shoulders. Claire paused at the street so Randall could dismount and close the gate behind them. *Closing the castle walls*, Jodie thought. He adjusted the backpack, climbed onto the machine again, and Claire headed west out of town.

"Long live the Queen," Jodie whispered.

She watched until the sound of the engine faded, then let the curtain drop and went to worry somewhere else.

CHAPTER FOURTEEN

WHEN CLAIRE arrived at Spence Alley, Guy was waiting on his porch with three men and a woman. She'd never seen any of them before, but she assumed they were his neighbors. She pulled the sledge around next to the house to leave the road clear for Michael's helicopter. Guy was down off the porch before she killed the sledge's engine.

"What's with the block party?" she asked as she and Randall got off the machine.

"I figured you'd be needing all the help you can get. I told them what you told me, and they're all willing to lend a hand. Whatever you need."

Claire said, "I appreciate that." She raised her voice so everyone could hear. "But right now, the best help you can give us is to go back into your homes and let us do our jobs. These are dangerous men, and we don't want to worry about someone getting caught in the crossfire."

The woman said, "We know what these guys have been doing. We want to help bring 'em down."

"I appreciate that anger, ma'am. Like I said, the more people who get involved, the more dangerous it will be."

She grimaced but stepped back from the edge of the porch.

"Hopefully we'll be back here within the hour, and we're going to need a place to keep those women safe while we wait for our ride. If you truly want to help, make coffee or tea or hot cocoa. Have enough soup or stew on-hand that they can all eat their fill. They probably haven't had a whole lot of good home-cooking and they're going to be craving something hot after being in a cold house for so long."

The residents were already moving back to their own homes. Guy's shoulders were hunched, and he looked sheepish.

"I just thought maybe a posse..."

"The thought is very much appreciated," Claire said. "But I think it's best to keep our numbers low. And I'm not lying about the food and drink. The women will be insanely grateful for that when we get them back."

"Then I guess I should start something brewing." He went back up onto his porch. "Good luck, Sheriff Curran."

She nodded, looked at Randall to make sure he was ready, then unholstered her gun. She gestured the way with her head and started walking. Randall made sure the backpack was settled properly, took out his own weapon, and followed her into the woods.

***

She was prepared for the women to have already gone to bed and couldn't hear her quiet knock on the back door, but there was a response almost immediately. Claire muscled the door open and went inside with Randall close behind. Stefaniya was the one who let them in, and she backed away when she saw Claire wasn't alone.

Claire held up her hands. "He's a friend. I trust him. This is Randall. It's okay."

The house was completely dark save for two lanterns in the living room. It looked as if the women had made a nest against an interior wall where they could huddle for warmth. A book was lying face down on the floor next to the pile of blankets. The women were now gathered at the door of the kitchen and Stefaniya went past them to look out the front window.

Tereza said, "We may not have much time. They have not brought us dinner yet."

"Seriously?" Randall said. "It's really late."

Claire motioned for the backpack. "They'll mention it in the Yelp review." She put the bag on the table and unzipped it. "We have coats, socks, and shoes. Hopefully, we have something close to everyone's size, but don't worry about perfect. This is just to get you through the snow to safety. The plan is to leave here, go through the woods, and then you'll wait in a safe house while we wait for a helicopter to come in and take you somewhere safe."

"Helicopter?" Kseniya said.

Vera said something in another language, her hands miming. Kseniya looked frightened but nodded.

"What about Mila?" Vera asked. "We will not leave without her."

"Russell will get her out once the four of you are safe."

Vera didn't look convinced by that plan. "We won't leave her," she said again.

"I know," Claire said. "But we're very low on ideal options, Vera. Getting the four of you to safety is our top priority. Once that's done, we'll be free to focus entirely on Mila."

"We~"

"He's coming," Stefaniya said, backing away from the window. "One of the men is coming."

"Shit." Claire met Randall's eye and they had a brief moment of silent communication. "Ladies, everyone into the kitchen. Back wall, crouched down. Now! Go."

They hurried off. Randall said, "You~"

"Keep them covered."

He nodded and followed them into the kitchen. Claire crossed the living room in two striding steps and ducked behind the door just as it swung open.

"Hello, hello, girls!" Claire recognized Jesse's voice. "Sorry it took so long for..."

Jesse had stopped a few steps inside the door, staring at the empty room. He turned to look at the bedroom, clearly assuming they'd gone to sleep already. Claire pushed the front door closed. He turned toward the sound, bringing his jaw around to meet Claire's fist, already in motion. He dropped the tray of food when he stumbled backward, plates and silverware clattering across the floor. She crowded him, sweeping his back foot with her leg so that he fell hard onto his back.

"You're gonna~"

She shoved him onto his stomach and pulled one of his arms back. "You're under arrest. Anything you say~"

He bucked hard, twisting and shooting his elbow back at her. Claire avoided the blow, but he managed to squirm out of her grasp and get on his back.

"You!"

He lashed out with both fists but Claire easily avoided the sloppy attack and grabbed his wrist again. With her free hand, she unhooked the taser from her belt and jabbed it into his stomach. One squeeze of the trigger took all the fight out of him. His feet kicked the floor and he rocked his head back, crying out in pain and surprise. Claire rolled him again and put a knee in the middle of his back.

"As I said, you have the right to remain silent..."

She cuffed him as she finished reading his rights. When she was finished, she used his belt and shirt collar to pull him upright. Randall came out of the kitchen and she pointed at the laundry room. Randall opened the door and Claire took their prisoner inside. She put a hand on his shoulder, pressing him to the wall, and patted him down with her other hand.

"You do not want to make Mr. W any angrier at you than he already is, lady," Jesse said. "Trust me, that is one guy you don't want on your bad side."

"I've seen a lot of bad guys with a lot of bad sides." Claire found a phone in Jesse's pocket. "It rarely works out well for them."

She pushed him into a sitting position and motioned for Randall to stand guard. She turned on Jesse's phone, expecting she would need a passcode, but it opened with a swipe of her thumb.

"You're not a very good criminal, are you, Jesse?"

Vera had ventured forward and peeked into the laundry room. "You actually... you did it. You stopped him."

"One down," Claire said, scrolling through Jesse's contacts. "Actually this is three down. We're halfway there."

Jesse had messages from all six of the men, letting her confirm the names she'd accumulated for them. The most recent message was from Tim. She couldn't remember if she'd dubbed him Dopey or Bashful. She tapped on the screen and read the last string of messages, all of which had been sent the night before.

JESSE: You don't have to go over there all the time and see them! It's fuckin crazy! I didn't think they were all that hot at first, you know, but after a while

TIM: Any port in a storm?

JESSE: lol absolutely!!! Too bad bossman would skin us alive if we actually did anything.

TIM: Sometimes I'm almost ready to risk it

JESSE: Suicide lol

Claire grunted and looked at the window, then at the dark laundry room door. Randall was watching Jesse, but also had an eye on her, waiting for word on what their next move would be. Claire went into the kitchen. The women, other than Vera, were still crouching on the floor.

"Shoes and coats, ladies. Quick."

Randall said, "What's the plan, boss?"

"They're going to notice he's gone eventually. Vera, how long does he usually stay over here when he brings you dinner?"

"Sometimes not long. Sometimes a few minutes. Never longer than ten."

Claire said, "They'll know something is wrong when he doesn't come back."

She tapped the phone against her hand. The plan was to lead the women back to Spence Alley, let Randall deal with Wyman and the remaining thugs. She looked at Jesse, who glared back at her. He was six foot, maybe three hundred pounds, and she'd been lucky to sucker punch him the way she did. She was tough but in a fair fight, things might have turned out very differently. Randall was a shade over six feet, lean but strong.

"What are you thinking, boss?" he asked.

"I'm thinking Jodie is going to make herself a widow when she finds out this was my idea. But we need to get this guy out of here. I'm pretty sure I could handle him on the walk through the woods, but if I had to choose who would be his escort..."

Randall lowered his voice. "You swore to Jodie you'd leave."

"Yeah," Claire said. "But I didn't know we'd have a prisoner. That changes things. I'll be left with three of them to handle."

"That's still a lot."

"Better than four," she said. "If you take that guy with you. We have an opportunity here. We need to take it."

Randall pressed his lips together and shook his head. The women had finished putting on their shoes and were bundled in coats.

"Is Jodie the type to kill the messenger...?"

"Just make sure there are witnesses around."

Randall sighed in defeat. "Fine. Okay. What's your plan?"

Claire held up the phone. "I'm going to play To Catch a Predator."

"Gross."

"Yeah, I expect I'll need a couple showers to get it off me when I'm done. But it's a surefire way to lure one of the guys over here. Then I'll only have to worry about Wyman and one other guy. The odds are getting better all the time."

Randall said, "You *like* those odds? Remind me to play blackjack against you sometime." He took the cuffs from his belt and gave them to her, replacing the ones on Jesse's wrists. "Play for money. Lots and lots of money."

He used one of the extra pairs of socks to gag Jesse, then draped one of the coats over his shoulders and zipped it up with his arms trapped inside. The coat also had a hood, which he pulled over Jesse's head and cinched the drawstring tight.

Vera watched, then marched over to Claire. "I would like to stay and help."

Claire shook her head. "I can't allow that. But thank you."

Vera looked like she wanted to argue, but decided to surrender. "Good luck, Sheriff Curran."

"Thank you."

Randall handed Vera a flashlight. "Wait until we're in the woods to switch it on. Then follow our footprints in the snow straight west. It'll take us right where we need to go." He put one hand on Jesse's left shoulder, gripped his right bicep with the other, and marched him forward. To Claire, he said, "Be careful."

"You too."

"Move it," he said to Jesse, and shoved him ahead as if he was being used as a human shield.

Tereza opened the back door and froze on the threshold as she looked out into the darkness. Vera came up behind her, touched her shoulder gently. Kseniya reached out and took Tereza's hand in hers. Stefaniya stood behind the three of them, tall and strong, preventing anyone from forcing them to take this step before they were ready. Finally Tereza exhaled in a puff of white smoke and stepped out into the night. Kseniya and Vera went with her, and Stefaniya followed, turning to look at Claire and Randall before she was out of sight.

"Give 'em hell, Lance," Randall said.

Claire followed him to the door and watched as they disappeared single-file into the woods. Once they were gone, she took out Jesse's phone and scrolled back over his texts with Tim to learn his voice well enough to mimic it. When she felt confident, she tapped to compose a new message.

Dude you won't believe it. These chicks are REDDY. Its fuckin freezing over here, and they'll do anything to keep warm.

She added a few emojis she hoped were suggestive and hit send. A few seconds later, she got a reply.

lol your insane. You need to get laid, man, for real.

Claire grimaced and sent back *I'm about to!* She felt disgusting. *Get over here and get yours! I can only do so much!*

ripe for the picking right lol but boss finds out, we're toast
Plenty we can do without leaving evidence, man. There practically climbing all over me!! Backup lol.
oh man, I hate you.

She went to the window and looked out. A minute passed, then two. If she'd just channeled a horny asshole for no reason, she doubted there would be enough showers in the world to make her feel clean. How much could she push this? Could she send another message asking him to come over? At what point would he become suspicious? She remembered now that Tim was Bashful, the soft-spoken one who didn't say much. If he was too shy or~

The front door of the main house opened. The man who came out was short, barrel-shaped, and rolled his shoulders when he walked. He made her think of gorillas at the zoo as they strutted up to gaze out at the people gawking at them. In the short time it took him to get from one house to the other, he looked over his shoulder three times to make sure no one was watching him.

Claire moved behind the door again. This time she already had the taser in hand when the door opened. Tim slipped inside, shutting the door behind him. He was so focused on the bedroom door that he might not have noticed her even if the lights had been on. Tim moved stealthily toward the bedroom and Claire silently fell into step behind him.

"Jesse?" he whispered. "You in there, man? Can I have the tall mean one?"

"Am I tall and mean enough for you?"

He yelped and spun around. Claire hit him in the chest hard enough to knock the wind out of him, preventing any cries for help he might have made. He backpedaled and hit the wall.

"You!" he wheezed.

"I keep getting that," Claire admitted. "Face the wall."

He obeyed, to her surprise. "I-I-I wasn't going to do anything they didn't want."

"Consent is real important to you, huh?" she said.

"I'm not a rapist." There were tears in his voice.

Claire said, "Yeah. You were just going to have sex with a couple of women you were keeping prisoner, all of whom were reliant on you for their basic necessities. But you were going to make sure they gave consent before you did anything."

"Please," he said. "Please, please, I can't... I can't go to jail for rape."

"Look on the bright side," she said. "Maybe all your other crimes will take up enough time that no one will bother going anywhere with the attempted sexual assault charge."

He sobbed. "Oh god..."

"Come on."

She walked him to the laundry room and put him on the floor. She patted him down and came up with another phone, a wallet, and a small knife. She held up the blade so he could see it.

"This probably helps with the consent, huh?"

"Oh god," he blubbered again.

She remembered seeing him in Rucker's photos, swaggering and powerful. Any bravado he may have had was gone now. He'd given in to a shameful urge and was being punished for it. The women he planned to victimize had vanished, replaced by a vengeful woman with the ability to make him pay for showing his true nature. She doubted he would cause much trouble, and she wanted to save her handcuffs for someone who presented a real threat, but she wanted to be certain he was contained.

"Coat, shoes, socks."

He looked up at her. "What...?"

"Your coat, your shoes, and your socks. If you're wearing layers, everything but the bottom shirt goes." She snapped her fingers. "Now! It was good enough for the women you were holding here."

He unzipped his coat and shrugged out of it. Claire waited as the pile of clothes grew bigger, finally leaving him in a plain white T-shirt.

"Belt, too."

This time he didn't hesitate. "I swear I wasn't going to force anyone to–"

"Ripe for the picking," Claire quoted from his text.

He blubbered and ducked his head. She crouched down and used the belt to bind his arms, pulling it tight enough to be uncomfortable without being cruel. It would force him to lie on his side instead of a more natural position, but she wouldn't lose any sleep about it. She balled up his socks and used them to gag him. She did feel a little bad about that, but then she remembered what he'd come over here to do, and her pity evaporated.

She gathered his clothes and took them into the kitchen. Randall had left behind the bag with the extra coats and shoes. She added Tim's clothes to it, zipped it up, and stowed it behind the fridge just in case Tim found his courage and got free. She went back to the living room window. All the lights in the main house were on, but she didn't see any movement in the windows. Only two men were left in the house, Wyman and Ryan. She hated that their names rhymed, so she switched Ryan to Dopey to make it sound better in her head.

The boss and one of his lackeys. She assumed she had five minutes before either of them noticed their missing pals, maybe three to five more after that before one of them came to investigate. Wyman wouldn't come himself, so Dopey would get the job of seeing what their compadres were up to. Pro, she had a taser, and con, she only had one pair of handcuffs. Not ideal.

Claire went to the back door and slipped outside. She assumed Tim was too deep in his self-loathing to even notice she'd left, but she would have to move quickly.

She went to the tree line and used it as cover to circle around behind the main house. The generator was there, tucked up against the wall like a stone. She crouched next to the machine and found the control panel. She assumed there was a process for safely shutting these things down, but she didn't have time and frankly didn't give a damn if she fried their engine. She found the off button and held it down until the engine wheezed to a stop.

The main house went dark.

The clearing fell immediately, eerily silent. She stayed crouched down and moved back toward the door. She stayed close to the wall and waited, already hearing voices from within. There were three concrete steps leading from the back door down to the ground, and Claire went to the far side of them assuming anyone who came out would be focused on the generator.

"~filled that damn thing," Wyman snapped.

"~probably just froze up," the last man standing replied. "It was Jesse's turn to take care of it."

"Well, Jesse ain't here right now, is he? Go take care of it. It's already fucking freezing in here."

Claire held her breath. The shadows were thick enough that she doubted anyone would see her even if they looked right at her, but she didn't want to take the chance.

Seconds ticked by. Finally, she heard footsteps and the rattle of the doorknob. It swung open and Dopey came out. He shined a flashlight at the generator, closed the back door, and grunted as he stomped down the stairs.

"Gonna skin that asshole alive, I swear…"

Claire closed the distance between them before he could reach the generator. She pressed the ice-cold plastic of the taser against the exposed skin of his neck, and his entire body went rigid. Both his hands went up on instinct, and his head ducked down. She knew his brain registered the touch as a gun barrel, but she was willing to ruin the illusion by zapping him if he made a move.

"What the shit…"

"Do you have a weapon on you?"

"Flashlight. That's it."

"Drop it."

He obeyed, tossing it into the snow while keeping his hands at shoulder-level. "The fuck you come from, lady?"

"On your knees," she said. "Lace your fingers behind your head."

"You really plan to take us all out one by one? Seriously? You got lucky with George, 'cause he was lazy, and your girl was brutal with Teddy. But you have no idea what you're up against."

Claire cuffed his wrists. "Yeah? Who's your money on? Jesse? Where do you suppose Jesse is right now? When did you last see him? Or maybe you think Tim has a chance. Good ol' Timmy. Looks tough, but that boy has a crying problem. Last I saw, he was blubbering like a baby. He's probably peed his pants by now."

Ryan tried twisting to look at her. "Who the hell are you, lady?"

"Sheriff Claire Curran." She hauled him back onto his feet. "And you're under arrest. Come on, walk with me."

She walked him back to the house where the women had been held. She was concerned about him calling out for help, but he surprised her when he finally did speak.

"Look," he said quietly, "what kind of deals are going to be on the table here?"

"You feel like you'd be negotiating from a strong position?" she asked.

He said, "I swore I would never go back to prison, and I'm definitely not going to take the fall for Dennis fucking Wyman. I want to be your best friend now. I've been keeping records, okay? The people who bring the girls, the contacts he has overseas. Russia, all over Asia... the guy keeps talking about how untouchable he is, but I kept track in case this day came, because of course it was coming."

Claire kept walking. They had reached the women's house.

"Look, you've clearly won. You know our names. Hell, I don't even know how you found this place. Den was insane about being sure we were never followed. That's why your pal got a bullet across the bow, because he~"

Claire shoved Ryan against the wall of the house and pressed her arm against his throat.

"His name was Callum Rucker. He was one of the best men I've ever known. And you assholes killed him like he was nothing. You want a deal? You want to be my friend? You have no idea how tempted I am to just tie you all up out here and let you slowly starve to death. There's going to be a time to talk about deals, I'm sure, but right now the only deal I'm willing to make is you shut up and I'll keep doing this by the book. Can you sign off on that deal, Ryan?"

He swallowed hard and nodded. "Yes, ma'am."

She let him go and shoved him forward. She yanked the door open and marched him inside. She could hear Tim in the laundry room, still sobbing. She told Ryan to wait as she pulled the back door tight into its warped frame and flipped the locks. She expected Wyman would eventually look outside, see the flashlight Ryan dropped, and then he'd do one of two things: hunker down with his hostage, or follow the footprints in the snow to here. There was no need to give him an easy way in.

Ryan was staring at the laundry room door. "Holy shit, I thought you were bullshitting. How'd you make him cry?"

"I can show you if you want. Go."

She took him into the bedroom. She took his shoes and belt, then unfastened one of the cuffs so he could take off his coat. She looped the chain around a pipe in the corner before she put the bracelet back on. He remained docile throughout, supporting his claim that he wanted to act as an informant. Claire gestured for him to sit, and he slid down the length of the pipe to lean against the wall.

"The woman in the main house," Claire said. "What room is she in?"

"Kitchen. Dennis would probably be in the living room, but he probably realizes something's up by now. So I can't swear what he's doing. The house looks pretty much like this, except kind of sideways. The rooms are all on that wall." He gestured vaguely. "Reversed, you know?"

"Yeah. Okay."

She started to leave, but he stopped her. "Sheriff, wait." She turned to look back. He showed her his palms. "This might come off as a threat, but it really is just a warning. Dennis fucking hates your guts. No one has ever made him work this hard, and he resents it coming from some small-town nobody. He's going to come at you, no holds barred. I'm just saying if you have to fight dirty, it might save your life."

Claire said, "Noted."

She closed the bedroom door on him. She took out her phone and dialed Randall's number as she crossed to the living room window and looked out. Everything was quiet and dark.

"Boss?"

"Two more down," she said, "one to go."

"Damn," Randall said. "Everyone here is safe at Guy's. The biggest threat right now is overdosing on stew."

Claire managed a smile at that. "Good to know. Tell them to sit tight. Their ride should be coming along soon."

"Everything is pretty much locked down here, boss. If you needed backup..."

"Thanks, Randall. But those women need someone they can trust. Guy has been reliable, but he's still a stranger to them. They need the badge."

He sighed. "I guess that's logical."

"Hopefully Jodie will agree."

"Be careful, Claire."

"Will do."

She hung up, stared at the phone, and dialed Michael Hood-Colby's number. He answered on the first ring.

"Sheriff. I'm sitting in the bird, ready to go. Paige is here, too. She decided having me fly her chopper was riskier than the weather. Hopefully, her being here doesn't affect the plan too much."

"No, it actually might be good for another woman to be flying the getaway car." She looked outside to make sure Wyman wasn't sneaking up on her. "We're almost ready for you. But there's been a slight change to the plan..."

CHAPTER FIFTEEN

CLAIRE OPENED the front door of the house and stepped outside, crossing the snowy front lawn. She walked to the center of the road, boots crunching through the thin layer of ice that had formed on top of the drifts. The snow was still mostly powder, though, and it accumulated on her feet and the bottom half of her uniform slacks. She stopped in the middle of the wide road and turned to face the main house.

"Dennis Wyman!"

Her voice bounced off the empty houses to either side, returned to her by the trees clustered behind them. The air was completely still, the wind blocked by the same echoing trees. Her gun was in her hands, aimed at the ground, ready to be brought up with no hesitation. She was in a shooter's position, feet planted shoulder-width apart, eyes locked on the front door of her adversary. The quiet helped her focus on her surroundings so she was confident no one would sneak up behind her without the snow giving them away.

"This is Sheriff Claire Curran of the Squire's Isle Police Department. You are under arrest. Exit the house with your hands up."

She could hear a clock ticking in her head. When she got to forty-seven, the front door opened and Dennis Wyman stepped outside. He was smiling, eyebrows up but his small eyes still squinted shut. He looked like a man who was caught sleeping when UPS rang his doorbell. He stepped out onto the porch, stared at her, then came down the steps at a casual pace. She brought the gun up and leveled it at his chest. He reared back, faking shock.

"I think there's been some kind of misunderstanding, Sheriff."

"Stop where you are. Put your hands on the back of your head."

He stopped, but held his hands out to either side. "Where are my friends? I assume you were picking them off...? I gotta tell ya, that was slick. That was real slick. I'm almost impressed."

"Hands," Claire said. "Back of your head."

He took a slow step forward. "Claire Lance," he said, then whistled and shook his head. "There's all kinds of stuff about you. If even half that shit actually happened, I'm a fan. Truly. I respect a lot of what you did. That ledger you exposed in Seattle? Those were some disgusting assholes, and you did this world a service by making sure they got what was coming to them."

"You have the right to remain silent. Start now."

Wyman grinned. He took another step. "You must know a lot about me, too. Like the fact that nothing sticks to me. That's not because I always win every battle. It's because I'm smart enough to know when to retreat. So I'm willing to make you an offer, out of respect for who you are. We're at an impasse. I'm going to surrender. This island is convenient, sure, but it's not worth the damn trouble. I'm willing to walk away. You want the island, it's yours. You win."

"Anything you say can be held against you in a court of law," Claire said. "You have the right to an attorney..."

"Or one will be appointed to me," Wyman said with a condescending smirk. "Don't worry, I can afford attorneys."

She realized she'd been hearing a rhythmic thumping for the past few seconds, but now it had grown loud enough it couldn't be ignored. She saw Wyman's smile falter, his eyes dipping to the left and then the right, clearly trying to figure out what he was hearing. The thumping was loud enough now that she had to raise her voice to be sure her voice carried over it.

"Do you understand these rights?"

His mask fell, his eyebrows knitting together as his smile slid away like oil spilling off his face.

"Fine. No more games."

He twisted to reach behind his back. He was mid-draw when the helicopter descended through the canopy directly above them. Claire kept one hand on her gun and used the other to tug her knit cap down over her face. The eyeholes were askew, but she could see well enough for what needed to be done. A spotlight switched on, flooding the road like a miniature sun as the downdraft from the rotors created a massive blizzard from the powder all around them.

"How long will it take you to get from the airport to Spence Alley?" Claire had asked Michael on the phone.

"Paige says three minutes, max."

"Leave in two minutes," Claire said. *"Before you get to Spence Alley, I want you to drop down on the street just east of it. Don't land, just put on the spotlight and let the rotors kick up the snow."*

"*You're basically going to turn the whole road into a snow globe if we do that,*" Michael warned.

"*That's what I'm counting on.*"

She couldn't have planned for them to arrive just as Wyman pulled a gun, but she wasn't going to question such perfect timing. Wyman brought one hand up to cover his face from the blinding light, as well as the icy shards that were now pelting every inch of exposed skin. Claire ran at him. He brought his gun up and aimed blindly, but Claire dodged with ease before he even pulled the trigger. She barreled into him, wrapping her arms around his trunk and hauling him down.

The helicopter gained altitude, continuing on its rescue mission. Wyman grabbed Claire's throat with both hands, which was technically a good thing since it meant he'd dropped his gun. His grip was tight but not quite enough to choke her. She pressed her gun into his stomach hard enough to be sure he felt it, stared into his eyes. The sound of the helicopter was still loud, but not as deafening as it had been seconds earlier.

"You pulled a weapon on me, Mr. Wyman. This ends, right here and now. You already admitted defeat. The only thing left is figuring out how the ending goes."

He dropped his hands, his smile returning. "Well, hell."

Claire pushed up off of him, hauled him up by the front of his shirt, and gestured with the gun. "Hands on top of your head. Fingers laced together."

He used exaggerated movements to comply with her orders. He smirked at her with his hands on the back of his head like he was relaxing on a couch.

Then he rocked his head forward, cracking his skull against hers.

Claire cursed and stumbled back as blood poured down over her left eye. She could still see well enough to catch Wyman drop into a crouch and grab the gun he'd dropped.

"Wyman! *Stop!*"

He brought the gun up. Claire's first shot threw his shoulder back. He returned fire and Claire felt something sting her right arm. She emptied her clip as she approached him, a bullet for every step. By the time she reached him, Wyman was flat on his back in the snow. Every shot had found its mark, but she didn't care to catalogue them at the moment. She looked at her own arm, relieved to see that there was little more than a tear in the sleeve and a nasty-looking slice on the bicep. There was a lot of blood, it might end up needing stitches, but it would heal.

She holstered her weapon and stepped over Wyman's body. She could hear sobbing before she even reached the main house. She climbed the steps and stood in the doorway.

"Mila? My name is Claire Lance. I'm here to take you home."

She stepped inside, unaware she'd said the wrong name until later, but at the moment it didn't matter. The house was an icebox, dark and foreboding. She paused in the living room to pinpoint the origin of the crying.

"Mila?" she said again. "Do you remember me? We saw each other through the window."

"Police woman?"

Claire moved toward the laundry room. Apparently, she wasn't the only one who saw its potential as a makeshift cell.

"That's right. You don't have anything to worry about."

"The men~"

"They're gone. All of them. Most of them are in custody, and Dennis Wyman is dead. My job now is to get you to safety."

She opened the laundry room door. Mila was huddled against the far wall. She had her arms protectively raised over her head. Claire was suddenly very glad she hadn't let Randall do this part of the mission. She crouched down and offered her hand. Mila stared at it. Finally, she reached out.

"Thank you, Miss Police."

She smiled. "You can just call me Claire."

***

Michael delivered Randall and the women to the hospital, then flew back to pick up the second group. Claire put Ryan up front, since he was at least pretending to be cooperative, and sat Tim behind him. She put herself between Tim and Mila. The girl was nervous about the idea of flying and leaned over to nervously whisper to Claire as Michael prepared to take off.

"May I hold your hand when he goes up?"

"You can hold it as long as you want."

Claire held her hand out, and Mila squeezed it. Guy and his neighbors were standing a safe distance away to witness the departure. They were all bundled in borrowed clothes, scarves, and caps. Michael checked that everyone was ready before he pulled up. Wyman's body had been left behind, abandoned until they had a better extraction plan. She took the time to move him into the main house and cover him with a blanket so he wouldn't be bothered by wild animals, but that was more for their sake than his. She had no idea what diseases he might give them.

They were above the trees in seconds, and Michael turned them back toward town. It looked like a Christmas card; the streets were plowed but fields of pristine white snow still lay over every lawn and public space. The windows of every house glowed with an inviting white or yellow aura. Just beyond the gingerbread town, the iced-over harbor glistened like it had been filled with diamonds. It was like flying over a fairytale.

Mila leaned over again, but this time she had to shout to be heard over the rotors. "The other women. They are okay?"

"They're at the hospital," Claire shouted back, squeezing Mila's hand.

Michael landed at the hospital a few minutes later. Randall, Harvey Moses, and Ami Konnerup were waiting at the emergency entrance with a trio of doctors. Claire was the first off the helicopter, ushering Mila down with her. She introduced Mila to Ami, who took her over to the doctors who would convince her to come inside for a check-up. Claire watched to make sure she was going with them before she turned her attention to the prisoners.

Randall had Ryan, while Harvey Moses handcuffed a still-whimpering Tim so he could be properly taken into custody.

"Wyman?" Randall asked.

Claire shook her head. "Not an issue."

Randall looked at her arm.

"Just a graze."

"Claire... you should know..."

"*Claire.*"

She turned to see Jodie running at her. "Ah, shit."

Randall spoke quickly. "I did not call her. She was listening for the chopper and followed it to the hospital. I've never seen a person so disappointed and angry to see me. It was bone-chilling."

Jodie had reached them. Her attention was, of course, immediately on the bloody patch on Claire's upper arm. She'd done her best to staunch the bleeding by wrapping a piece of cloth around her bicep, but it hadn't done much good.

"You got *shot?*" Jodie said.

"Grazed," Claire said.

"You *stayed behind.*"

"I had to." She kept her voice calm. "I'm sorry, but I had to. It was the right call."

Jodie worked her jaw. Her eyes were wide, catching the dim light. "I know," she said finally. "I know. You wouldn't have done it otherwise. But I'm going to be mad about it anyway. That's not fair to you, but~"

"No, I know. I get it. How long do you think you'll be mad?"

Jodie worked her jaw and looked past Claire. "Three days."

Claire nodded. "That's not so bad. I can manage three days."

The tension faded from Jodie's shoulders. When the anger vanished from her eyes, the only thing left was fear and relief.

"Starting tomorrow."

She threw her arms around Claire so suddenly that from the outside it could have looked like an attack. Claire returned the hug with equal force, despite the fact it hurt her arm. It soothed every other hurt she'd accumulated during the night, and she wasn't going to let go until she absolutely had to.

"Are they all safe?"

"The ones who were on the island, yes," Claire said.

"You got all the bad guys?"

"I did."

Jodie sniffled. "Good. Good, good..."

Claire held her. The doctors had gotten Mila inside, and her deputies had taken the prisoners into custody. Michael and Paige were still seated in the helicopter, clearly uncertain if they were allowed to just leave or if they needed to stay and give a statement. Claire could have let them off the hook, but that would mean ending the hug. She could have gone inside where it was warmer, and she felt completely frozen to the core, but that also would have meant the hug would end. With three days of anger to look forward to, it wasn't a sacrifice she was willing to make.

CHAPTER SIXTEEN

WHEN THEY finally went into the hospital, Rachel Crawford was at the closest nurse's station trying to look as if she hadn't been waiting for them.

"Doctor," Claire said. "Sorry for all the commotion here today."

"Oh, don't be. It's breaking up the monotony of people who slipped on the ice. One of the women asked to speak with you as soon as you arrived." Her eye drifted down to Claire's arm. "I can take you to her after I take a look at that."

Claire said, "That can wait."

Jodie pressed two fingers into Claire's side. "You want those three days to start right now...?"

"Right. Treatment first."

"Good." Jodie leaned in and kissed Claire's cheek. "I'll be down here in the waiting room when you get done."

Rachel led Claire to an exam room. She glanced back and let Claire enter first. "Three days...?"

"It's a wife thing."

"Ahh, got it. Say no more."

Even though she assumed she knew the answer, Claire asked, "Which of the women asked for me?"

"Vera. She seems to have assigned herself protector of the others."

Claire nodded. "That's the impression I got." She sat on the bed and unbuttoned her uniform blouse, shrugging it off her shoulders to carefully extract her wounded arm. "How are they doing?"

"Shell-shocked." Rachel pulled a cart over and rolled up the sleeve of Claire's undershirt. "I don't think they truly believe they're out of danger.

One of them, um... Kissy?"

"Kseniya," Claire said.

"Mm. She's asking a million questions. What's this town called, what state is it in, what is Washington known for, are we near Mount Rushmore or the Grand Canyon. I have one of my nurses up there answering everything for her. We put them in separate rooms. I thought they might like a little privacy after everything they've been through."

Claire nodded. "That's probably the right call for now. But if there's any way they can all sleep in the same room tonight..."

"I've already thought of it. We're making arrangements right now. And I have very good news for you, too. You won't have to lie to your wife about how serious this injury is."

"Really?"

"Yeah, it's a bleeder, but it'll be just fine. I won't even bother with stitches unless you want me to."

"I'll pass. Thanks, Doc."

Rachel treated the wound and gave it a proper bandage. "You know, speaking of wives, Alex probably won't tell you this straight out. She'll act all professional and treat you like a colleague. But she's really glad that you're in charge. She loved Rucker, and she respected him as a sheriff, and if anyone has to fill his shoes, she's glad it was you. She likes you a lot, Claire. Don't let her play tough girl on you."

"I appreciate the heads-up."

Rachel escorted her to a room at the end of the hallway and left her at the door. Claire knocked and stepped inside to find Vera in a white sweatshirt and blue scrub pants, standing at the window looking outside. She glanced over her shoulder to see who had come inside, then looked back out. Claire could see a tall streetlight on the corner, and it looked like a very gentle snow had started falling.

"This is real place?" Vera asked.

Claire smiled. "I thought the same thing when I first got here. It's definitely real."

Vera turned away from the window. "It reminds..." Whatever she was going to say got lost when she saw Claire's sleeve. "You were hurt?"

"He got the worst of it, believe me."

"And Mila?"

"She's fine. She's getting checked out in another room. Dr. Crawford said that they're making arrangements so you can all share a room tonight if you want. Or you can stay here if you'd prefer privacy. We want to make sure you're completely comfortable."

Vera walked to the bed. "Thank you. I think it would be better if we were all together. At least for tonight."

"Sure. Did they get you food, water...?"

"We have been taken in care," Vera said. "I... I have to confess to you."

Claire frowned. "For what?"

"When you came to us. The first day. I was going to tell the men about you. I was scared. Of course I wanted to be free, but also safe. And I thought you were dangerous. I thought you would fail. I thought it would be better to make the men happy by telling them about you."

"Oh," Claire said. "I understand that. You were in an impossible situation. If you think it requires absolution, consider yourself forgiven."

Vera was staring intently at the floor. She nodded. "Thank you."

"I'm going to check on the other women. If you want me to come back..."

"No. But wait." She went to the bedside table and uncovered a tray. She retrieved a chocolate chip cookie and brought it to Claire. "You had a long night. And you lost blood. Take this."

Claire smiled. She wanted to refuse, just on principle, but the gesture was too kind. It also felt like an extension of the apology. So she took the cookie and nodded.

"Thank you, Vera."

She took a bite of her cookie as she left the room. It was delicious, and she realized how little she'd had to eat that day. She looked down the hallway. The lights had been dimmed due to the lateness of the hour, but the rooms around Vera's shone brightly. Claire knew if she'd spent endless days in that horrible little house, she'd want to turn on all lights, too. She wanted to check on all the ladies, make sure they were okay, but there was something she had to get out of the way first.

She went to the third floor where Teddy Packard was still being held. One of her deputies, Chip Ewing, was sitting in front of the door with his phone out. He was young, with a young man's first mustache clinging to his upper lip, and it curled when he smiled.

"I have a bone to pick with you. Did you really give me babysitting duty while you and Old Man White got to play John McClane out in the woods?"

"Does Randall know you call him 'Old Man White'?" she asked.

"You should hear what I call him to his face."

Claire smirked. "I promise, next time there's a crazy shoot-out, you'll be my first call." She looked him up and down. "Then again, you're pretty puny for a human shield."

"Is this how you talk to your troops?"

"Yep," she said, stepping around him to let herself into Teddy's room.

Claire switched on the light, waking him. He grunted, then groaned and writhed in pain. He put a hand to his jaw and glared at her. She ignored him, went to the chair that was against one wall, and pulled it closer to the bed so she could put her boots up on the mattress when she sat down. She popped the last bit of the cookie in her mouth and chewed carefully as she settled in.

"Sorry, Teddy. I'd have offered you a bite, but... eh, you know."

He glared at her, but she could see the confusion in his eyes. He looked at her sleeve. She could see the gears working in his mind.

"Wyman's dead."

His eyes shot back up to her face, looking for signs of a lie. She didn't blink.

"One of your buddies... I probably shouldn't say which one... decided his best option was to offer information. You know cops, we love information. But you know, we don't like to take things on faith. We verify as much as we can. Then we can give the deal to whoever gives us the best information. It's a whole give and take thing."

She held his stare.

"I thought I would give you the opportunity of making a counter-offer, since you wound up getting the worst of anyone. Well, except Dennis, of course. You talk, give us good and actionable information, we might be willing to cooperate with you." She waited a second, then quickly stood up, pushing the chair back. "Then again, you're the guy who tried to abduct my wife, so you can get fucked as far as I'm concerned. Have a good night."

She was all the way to the door before he grunted, "Waaai..."

Claire turned to see his face twisted with pain from the effort of speaking. "What was that, Teddy? Did you say something?"

He swallowed hard. "Wha... kin'a... in-f'r-m...sh'n...?"

She walked back into the room. She had a pen in her pocket and found a pad of paper next to the bed. She dropped them on his chest.

"Start writing and let's see where we get."

***

By the time she finished getting Packard's written testimony, it was after midnight. She spent a few minutes with each of the rescued women, but they were all eager to have their first night of truly restful sleep, and Claire had no interest in delaying that. She made sure the women knew the deputies would stay in the hallway all night. "They're here for you," she reminded them. "They're your protection, not your jailors. If you need anything just ask and they'll make it happen."

Finally, at some unknowable time in the morning, she headed back downstairs to the lobby. Jodie was in on a long bench that ran along the wall next to the nurse's station. Claire started to say hello before she realized her wife was asleep despite the fact she was sitting up. Claire sat next to her and let the tension seep out of her spine. It felt like her legs evaporated, but her left arm felt like it weighed a thousand pounds. Her right arm was finally starting to sting.

She had only been seated for a minute when Jodie shifted toward her, instinctively laying her head on Claire's shoulder. Claire smiled and took

Jodie's hand in hers.

She was completely exhausted, desperate for sleep, but her brain refused to shut off. So she sat silently and listened to the muted sounds of a hospital at night. Some lights had been turned off while others glowed at half-power, creating odd shadows. A janitor's shoes squeaked down a hallway, and nurses swept from room to room like benevolent ghosts. It was peaceful if a little cold due to the bank of windows across from where they sat.

"Oh. Hey." Jodie stretched. "Earlier, while you were doing work stuff, I kept thinking about the mayor's daughter. Isabel. It made me wonder..."

Claire tried to keep her reaction neutral, but her voice still came out shocked. "You want a kid?"

"No!" Jodie sat up, eyes wide. "No, God, a *niece*. Babysitting, taking her out on boats or to the park. We have a playdate and then hand her back to her parents." She cupped Claire's cheek, holding back a laugh. "Oh, babe, your face. No, I don't want kids."

"Okay." Claire allowed her relief to show. "Yes, we can absolutely babysit once in a while."

Jodie put her head back down, still chuckling. "I didn't mean to give you a heart attack."

"You didn't, I just... I think this is a very good idea."

"Yeah, yeah," Jodie said. "God, I'm so tired..."

Claire knew why, knew how many sleepless nights Jodie had been suffering since this Wyman mess started. Now it was over and she could finally relax. She closed her eyes and tried to do the same. Claire wasn't sure how long she'd been sitting there with her eyes closed before she was startled by a blast of cold air. She tensed just enough to wake Jodie, whispering an apology to her as a woman strolled in through the emergency room doors.

She was a tall, willowy brunette bundled up in a puffy green jacket, scarf, and a knit cap. Her smile was wide and generous, though her eyes were apologetic as she approached them. She was carrying a to-go tray with two tall cups with the logo of Coffee Table Books on the sleeves.

"Sheriff," the woman said as she approached them. "I'm Kate Warren, with the *Register*. My editor insisted I come down and try to get an official statement from you. So here I am, against my will, to let you say 'no comment' to my face, and to give you and your lovely wife a cup of delicious coffee in the hopes you won't hate me."

Claire accepted the bribe. "I didn't think Coffee Table Books opened this early."

"One of my partners owns it."

"Oh right. Well... thank you, Kate. And if you don't mind waiting until I've finished it, I'd be happy to give you a statement."

Kate looked genuinely surprised. "My editor will be happy with the 'no comment.' You've clearly had a rough night."

"It's fine. Part of the job."

"Okay. If you're sure." She checked the fitness tracker on her wrist for the time. "I'll be in the cafeteria. Take as long as you want."

Jodie had put her head back down on Claire's shoulder. "Hi, Kate. You should also do a profile of her," she said sleepily. "A 'support your local sheriff' sort of thing."

"That's not necessary..." Claire said, but she could see the excitement on Kate's face. She surrendered. "But if you'd like to set something up, I'd be happy to."

Kate grinned. "For now, I'll just be happy with the story about why the helicopter was flying around in the middle of the night and why every cop in town is at the hospital. But like I said. When you're ready."

She left them, heading down one of the hallways.

When the sound of her footsteps faded, Claire said, "Did she say 'one of my partners'?"

"She's polyamorous," Jodie said. "With Amy and Nicole. Price is her professional name, but the three of them are the Warrens. You knew that."

"I guess I forgot." She rested her head against the wall. "Interview. Can't I just get shot again?"

Jodie said, "I thought you said it was just a graze."

Claire chuckled quietly. "You know, back when I used to do stuff like this, once things settled down, I would just quietly leave town. Move on. It feels weird to think I have to stay."

"You liked being a ghost."

"Mm." She brushed her thumb over the back of Jodie's hand. "There are perks to staying."

Jodie hoisted the cup Kate had brought her. "Free coffee?"

"Free coffee," Claire confirmed, tapping her plastic lid against the side of Jodie's cup.

She still had no idea what time it was. The sky outside was dark, but that could have been cloud cover concealing the dawn. She felt Jodie's head becoming heavy on her shoulder again.

"Joe."

"Mm?"

"Why are we sitting here? We can go home. Sleep in our own bed."

Jodie shifted. "We'd have to get up. Move. Don't wanna move." She kissed Claire's shoulder. "This bed is comfy enough."

Claire decided that was good enough for her. She smiled and put her head against the wall.

She had to admit, it was pretty damn comfortable.

EPILOGUE

Summer

THERE WAS no official day to mark the beginning of tourist season. The calendar didn't flip and, a day later, people from far and wide appeared en masse on the next ferry. It was a slow trickle, a marginal increase of visitors that someone with a trained eye could use as a bellwether. The past few days had seen more traffic violations than the previous month, so Claire knew they were on the brink of a new season. She parked at the ferry lanes in the hopes the sight of her would serve as enough of a warning to keep their visitors in line.

Patricia had found it very easy to convince the town council that the department deserved a bigger budget. As soon as the news broke about Wyman and everything the police had done, Claire could have requested a helicopter and a submarine and probably would have gotten it. In the end, she agreed to the new car to replace the firebombed one, and two new full-time deputies. Claire took the oldest squad car for herself and gave the new one to Randall and the other deputies. She'd taken a pay cut to accommodate the new hires, but she was still technically making more than she had as a deputy so she considered it a total win.

Two weeks after her shootout with Wyman, the Coast Guard descended on a cargo ship as it approached the Strait of Juan de Fuca. Officers discovered twelve women being held captive belowdecks, all of them with stories identical to the story Claire had heard in the cabin. The crew was taken into custody and, last she heard, they were making deals to lead law enforcement even higher up the ladder. She didn't dare hope they would end up catching every link in the chain, but at the very least they were increasing the pressure. Hopefully everyone involved would scatter like cockroaches and all their potential victims would be out of danger.

Vera, Tereza, and the rest of the women had been given a clean bill of health and released from the hospital. They were taken into the care of the US Justice Department, who moved at record speed to begin the process of getting them home. Claire had been surprised to get the first letter from Vera, but she soon started to look forward to them. She updated Claire with how everyone was doing, and their progress through the system. It was a slow process, and they were being housed in Olympia so they could testify against the men who'd held them prisoner, but all the signs pointed to them being back home by the end of summer.

After the furor died down, the island quickly went back to business as usual. She and Jodie settled back into the routine that was upended by the investigation. They went back home, put the Mustang back in storage, and found their groove again. The biggest change was that Jodie started calling every small inconvenience being grazed. Claire pretended to be annoyed, but she'd felt Jodie touching the scar when she thought she was asleep. If making such a close call into a joke was her way of coping, then Claire was willing to put up with it for as long as she needed.

Patricia scheduled an emergency election and, after a month with no one stepping up to run against her, Claire was officially named sheriff. Randall White was still her first deputy, her right hand man. Harvey Moses, her official replacement and first hire, spent most of his time patrolling on the north shore by Sholeh Harbor. Visitors left their cars to hike, sightsee, and go whale watching, leaving their cars behind unguarded. Last month he'd stopped four break-ins and caught a pickpocket.

The new third deputy position went to Ami Konnerup. She was young, new to the island, and eager to make a good impression. They got a depressing amount of domestic calls, and she liked having a female officer she could dispatch to those situations. Claire was worried some of the more senior volunteers would take issue with her getting the job, but she spoke with them and discovered they were happy with things the way they were.

In the end she had a department she could be proud of. She had a team she knew she could trust because they'd come through in what would probably be the toughest case they'd ever have. She didn't have the man who'd believed in her, who had taken a fugitive ghost and helped her find the police officer she'd always been meant to become. She still mourned Callum Rucker, and she was still looking for a way to appropriately honor the years of service he'd given to the island. For now, she would settle for honoring his memory by being a worthy successor to his title.

The radio chirped, and Minnie Culpepper's voice came through the speaker loud and clear. "Sheriff, you out there somewhere?"

Claire smiled and retrieved the handset. "I'm always on for you,

Minnie. What do you have?"

"If you're still parked by the ferry lanes, we just got a call from Gail's about a serial dine-and-dasher. Apparently, all the restaurants have been on the lookout for him since he's done it at least twice before, and Mr. Gail would like an officer on-site as soon as we can. You want to check it out?"

"Yeah, no problem." She looked in the side mirror. She could see Gail's from where she was sitting.

"You probably won't need the chopper for this one."

Claire rolled her eyes. "I used a chopper once, Minnie. *Once.*"

Minnie cackled. "You let me know if you need back-up. I'll head over there with my knitting needles."

"That's a ten-four, Min."

She hung up the microphone and got out of the car. She paused, then leaned back into the car to retrieve her cowboy hat. Randall had mocked her for it a little when she first started wearing it, and she occasionally drew a double-take from people she passed on the street, but it felt right. It felt like a part of the uniform. She put it on, pulled the brim low over her eyes, and headed for the stairs which would take her to the boardwalk outside Gail's.

The air coming off King's Harbor was crisp and cool, refreshing relief from the rising temperature of the afternoon. When she reached the top of the stairs, she walked over and rested her hands on the railing. The docks stretched out to either side and then out into the harbor, a small neighborhood with water instead of lawns, boat masts waving gently. A man was making repeated trips from the dock down to a private slip, carrying large packages from a pile down to his boat. Someone in a yellow kayak cut a slow line across the far side of the harbor. She heard the buzz of a plane overhead and tilted her head back, wondering if it was Michael at the controls, then returned her attention to the water.

King's Harbor. Squire's Isle, Lords and Ladies, the Knights softball team. Their island was very royal. It wasn't the largest kingdom, or the fanciest, but it was theirs, and it was worth fighting for. It deserved a defender who appreciated just how special it was.

"Sheriff!"

She turned toward the shout and saw a waiter in the open doorway of Gail's Seafood Shack. He pointed, and Claire followed his finger to a man running in the opposite direction. She pushed off the railing and gave chase.

Squire's Isle would always have threats. Some would be big, others would be minor. But as long as she was there, it would be protected.

Prize Fighter
Six years ago, professional boxer Max "Wrecker" Reszke lost control in the ring. One moment of blind rage put her opponent into a coma from which she never woke. Though cleared of any criminal charges, Max hangs up her gloves and swears that she'll never risk losing control like that again.

Until one night, a chance encounter in an alley, a damsel in distress. Max leaps into action and saves the stranger. She soon learns that the woman she saved is actress Renee Lamar. Renee, anxious and paranoid about security, offers to reward Max's chivalry with a job as her bodyguard.

Max has nothing to lose by agreeing, but soon discovers Renee might be her own worst enemy. Half a decade after leaving the ring, Max faces a new fight that can't be won with fists.

Into the Furnace
Kelly Lake comes from a family of firefighters, but she still had to prove herself to her brothers and her father before they accepted her as one of their own. On her days off she tends bar at the firehouse hangout across the street and spends time trying to breathe life into a relationship she knows is doomed. Her life is cruising along just fine until the day her squad responds to a horrific arson that will cause her carefully-orchestrated balancing act to come falling down around her. The blaze claims the lives of eleven people, half of them children, and the fire department takes the blame.

Kelly soon finds herself at the center of a media firestorm when she inadvertently becomes the poster girl for the incident. The trauma of the fire is compounded by her personal house of cards collapsing. Her relationship begins showing its cracks at the same time long-buried family secrets rear their ugly heads. Attacked from all angles, Kelly starts thinking the only place she'll be safe is running headlong into the furnace.

"Easily one of the best samplings of queer fiction I've had the pleasure to read in a very long time. I could not recommend it more, and sincerely hope that upon its release in November Into the Furnace will light the same fire in each of your hearts that it has already lit in mine." - Tabitha Beth, The Rainbow Hub.